KACI ROSE

Saving Noah

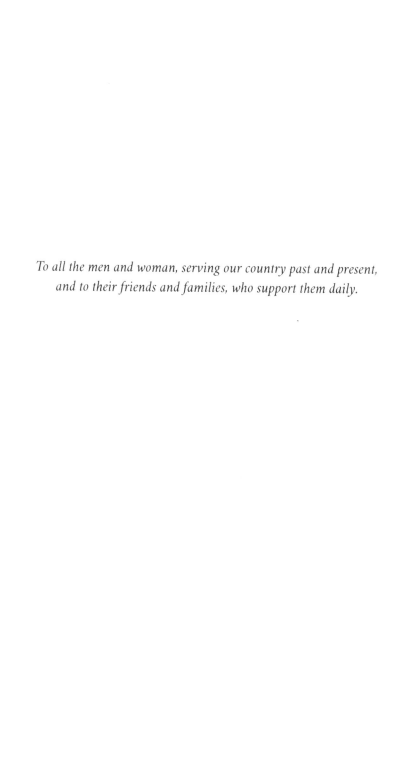

*To all the men and woman, serving our country past and present,*
*and to their friends and families, who support them daily.*

# Contents

# Blurb ·

*Can a scarred heart learn to love again?*
**Noah**

My unit was attacked, leaving every soldier with the option to fight our way out or die. I was one of the lucky few that made it, but not without battle scars. Half my body is scorched and blistered, the pain unbearable. I can't imagine anyone will want to look at me, much less be with me, after this, until I met Lexi. She came to visit her brother and stayed, when she realized I have no one. Now, all that gets me through the anguish of treatments and physical therapies is the chance to see her beautiful smile again.

**Lexi**

After fighting for their country, no soldier should have to suffer the painful healing alone. Yet, that's not what brings me back to Noah day after day. He's helping me work through the grief of losing my husband, but the day of his release is fast approaching. Our feelings for each other are undeniable. Will what's between us last outside the hospital walls, or will the emotional and physical scars we both carry destroy our chance at a fresh start?

This is a Steamy, Small Town, Military Romance. No Cliffhangers.

This is Book 1 in the Oakside Military Heroes Series.

As always there is a satisfying Happy Ever After.

If you love steamy romances with insta love, hot love scenes, military men, and small towns, then this one is for you.

# Get Free Books!

Do you like Cowboy? Military Men? Best friend's brothers? What about sweet, sexy, and addicting books?

**If you join Kaci Rose's Newsletter you get these books free!**

**Join Kaci Rose's newsletter and get your free books!**

Now on to the story!

# Chapter 1

**Lexi**

I hate hospitals.

That's what I'm thinking right now, as I stand in a waiting room at a military facility in Germany. I'm pacing and my sister-in-law, Becky, is sitting down, back ramrod straight, staring blankly at the wall.

We were at a family dinner with my parents when Becky got the call.

My brother is a Marine, and while he's been deployed, Becky comes over each week for family dinner. My parents insist on dinner every Sunday no matter what. Becky says it's been a great distraction during deployments.

Well, thank God we were there, when she got the call. She was told my brother had been hurt, but he was alive. They said it's serious and were taking him to a military hospital in Germany.

When she was so stunned that she wasn't able to speak, I had to take over the phone call and get all the details. The moment we hung up the phone, the house erupted in a flurry of activity.

There was no way we were letting her go alone. Since my dad just had back surgery a few weeks ago, he couldn't go, and my mom needed to stay to take care of him, so that left me. Just like that, we were packing our bags, more like I was packing both our bags, because Becky wasn't able to focus.

Becky may be my brother's wife, but she has been my best friend, since grade school. So, even if it wasn't my brother who was hurt, I'd still be right by her side.

My parents made me promise I'd call them the moment we landed, and again, after we talked to the doctors. My mom wants photos and video proof he's okay.

That was Sunday.

We took several connecting flights out of Savannah, Georgia to get on our flight to Germany. Neither of us slept. I don't think anyone on the plane could tell anything was wrong. If they did, they didn't say anything. We defaulted to our old selves, connected to the plane's Wi-Fi, turned on beauty tutorials on YouTube, and spent half the flight saying things like *'Why did they think that was a good idea?'* and *'What did she do to her hair?'*

But when they announced we were landing in Germany, we both became somber, feeling again like a bucket of cold water was poured over us. We landed, made it through customs, got to our hotel, and then checked in. That was what would have been Monday night back home. I think it's early morning Tuesday here though, but honestly, I'm not completely sure.

After dumping our stuff in our room, we headed right to the hospital. I'm not kidding less than sixty seconds in the room. That brings us to here. Now, we're waiting to be escorted in to see Johnny.

From what we have been told, his unit was on patrol and

2

was hit by an IED. We don't know any details other than he was alive, when he was transferred here. So, now we wait.

A nurse comes out about fifteen minutes later and leads us back through several sets of doors, and finally, to a large half circle room. The nurse's station is in the center, and there are about twelve beds arranged in a horseshoe around the nurse's station so the nurses can see every patient from their desk. From what the nurse says, this is the ICU room, but family is allowed here.

She leads us to Johnny's bed, and although he looks pretty beat up, he's fairly alert. He's in good spirits, but that's always been Johnny, happy-go-lucky. When he sees Becky, his face lights up. With tears in her eyes, she hugs him carefully.

Then, the nurse starts talking to us, like Johnny isn't even right in front of us.

"He has some burns and bruises, and we had to amputate part of his leg just below the knee, but he will be a good candidate for a prosthetic. There were some internal injuries, too. He will need significant recovery time and physical therapy, too. We're watching him now for infection, and as soon as he's in the clear, he can go back stateside. If you need anything or have any questions, check with us at the desk. The doctor will be by later."

I thank her and hang back, letting them have their moment, but I overhear the nurse talking about the guy in the bed next to Johnny. Apparently, he's been severely burned on the right side of his body, has a high risk of infection, and they don't know, if he will make it. He's been in and out of consciousness. When they say his name, my heart sinks.

*Noah Carr.*

I've seen Noah and his fiancée, Whitney, around different

events and deployment homecomings. I'm not a fan of his fiancé, but Noah has always seemed like a great guy, not that I ever talked to him in person.

Then, it all seems to hit me, and my eyes water. I refuse to think of that day. The day I got a very different visit. I say a prayer for the man in the next bed and hope he knows how lucky he is to be alive.

Instead, I try to focus on Johnny, and when his eyes meet mine, it's like he knows what I'm thinking. Holding his arms out to me, he wraps me in a hug.

"I'm not going anywhere, Lex. I promise you that." He whispers in my ear.

We sit with Johnny, and he asks us to talk about back home or anything, really. Becky tells him about family dinners, what is going on at work, and our dad's back surgery. It's all stuff I've heard over the last few weeks, and after a while, I zone out a bit and take a look around me.

When a woman enters the room, following a nurse, she captures my attention. She's all dolled up in a dress and heels, her makeup perfectly done, and not a hair out of place. Her shoes and bag all match her outfit in stark comparison to other family members, who like Becky and I, look like we just got off the plane and came straight here.

When she moves her hair from her face, I recognize her. It's Whitney, Noah's fiancée. Though, Noah appears to be awake, he's not talking. Looking at her, I don't hear what she's saying at first, but it's apparent that she's angry. I try not to eavesdrop, but as her voice gets louder, it's hard not, too.

Then, I hear what's she saying, and my heart sinks, but then, I'm furious.

"How the hell am I supposed to explain you to people? Burns

all over your face, and you'll ruin our wedding photos. How could I possibly marry you now? We could never have kids, because they'd be terrified of you, and they'd think you're a monster. We'd never be able to go out in public. What were you thinking going anywhere near that fire?"

When Noah turns his head away and locks eyes with me for the first time, we really see each other, and my heart stops. His eyes are sapphire blue, and I feel the air around us start to sizzle. I've never felt this jolt from someone just looking at me. When my heart starts up again, it's racing in overtime.

I look over at Johnny, who is their Unit Leader, and I can see he's pissed. I've only ever seen Johnny this angry once before in my life, and it ended very, very badly.

"We are done. There's no way I can marry you now," she says in a final blow and turns to walk out of the room.

Before I can even think, I'm right behind her, and she doesn't make it out of the door, when I'm in her face. One of the nurses is on the phone and watching us, like a hawk, and hopefully, calling security.

"You're a real piece of shit," I tell her. She looks like she's been slapped, but before she can speak, I go on. "If you didn't love him, why even come here? Why make the effort? He's fighting for his life, and that's how you talk to him? You're the monster not him. You know what? This is the best thing that could have happened to him, as it will weed people like you out of his life."

"You know nothing," she snarls and tries to move around me.

I block her path and give a sarcastic laugh, "I know you're lucky enough for him to live and make it home. Not everyone does." I say, walking away, as security meets her in the hall to escort her out.

One of the nurses gives me a smile, as I walk back into the room, but I keep going to Noah's bed. I'm on his good side, well, not the burned side, and standing here, I can see him, Johnny, and Becky.

Noah still isn't talking, and his eyes are barely open. When I lean in, I can tell his eyes are trying to focus on me.

"I don't know if you will even remember this, but you dodged a bullet with her. I know it hurts right now, but it's better to know her true nature than to be trapped in a marriage with someone as selfish and shallow. There's someone out there who will love you for you." I say.

He grunts but still doesn't say anything.

"Listen, we aren't all shallow and materialistic. Look at Becky. She fell in love with my brother, and it wasn't for his good looks."

I see Johnny flip me the bird, but Becky laughs.

"She's right," Becky says. "The right woman, not a girl like your ex there, but a real woman falls in love with the person. Looks fade, but the man inside doesn't."

I smile at him, "The right girl won't care about the scars, and she'll only care about you."

Being this close to him for the first time is intoxicating. It's like he's pulling me in. Though, he still hasn't said anything, his eyes are fixed on me. So, I figure this is the perfect time to tell him my favorite quote on scars.

"From every wound, there's a scar, and every scar tells a story. A story that says you survived. A scar simply means you were stronger than whatever tried to hurt you. Besides, scars are just tattoos with better stories, as they are God given tattoos."

6

When I reach for his hand, I'm not expecting the sparks that shoot up my arm. I did not anticipate the electricity, flowing between us. I figure it's got to be the adrenaline from telling his ex off, right?

"You *will* fight, and you *will* be okay. You don't have a choice." I say sternly.

Then, speaking for the first time, he looks at me again, and his words are slow. It's obvious that it takes a lot out of him just to talk. "What's the point? I don't have… anyone to fight with me… like Moore does. He has you two. No one came for me."

He's referring to Johnny, my brother, whose last name is Moore. Though, he's Johnny to me, it's still hard hearing the guys he's stationed with calling him Moore.

"*I* came for you," I reply to Noah.

Johnny gives me a nod, telling me it's okay, and that I made the right choice.

"Besides," I continue. "You will save me from being the third wheel over there."

Just then, a nurse comes around and gives him some more pain medicine. Since I know it will knock him out fast, I bend close to his ear.

"I'm not going anywhere. Fight for me and choose to live. I *will* be here when you wake up." I say.

He doesn't respond but is back asleep from the medicine, so I walk back over to my brother's bed.

"That's Noah, and I remember you talking about him, but what's his story?" I ask.

"Noah Carr. His parents are in Colorado, but they don't have the money to come out here, take time off, or even get passports. He sends money home to them every paycheck to help them and his two younger sisters out. Once he's stateside, I don't think they'll even be able to make it to visit." Johnny says.

I nod and turn to Becky, "We should take up a collection from The Unit back home, and see if we can raise the money to help get them out to visit, once he's stateside."

Becky nods, "I'll get working on it with the other wives."

I walk back over and sit down next to Noah and take my first good look at him. Though, I see very little of it, I can tell he has thick, curly, brown hair. Most of his head and face are bandaged, but I remember his piercing blue eyes.

Looking down at the bed, I see his right arm is bandaged, and I'm assuming his leg is as well.

Before long, how tired I am catches up with me. It's now some time Tuesday, and I haven't slept, since we got the call about Johnny. I fold my arms on the side of Noah's bed and rest my head on them. I just need to close my eyes for a few minutes.

# Chapter 2

**Noah**

I wake up, and my first thought is her. The beautiful blonde with gray eyes. I remember Moore talking about his sister, and how they were close. I vaguely remember seeing her at our last homecoming, but we didn't spend a lot of time together.

Why was she being so nice to me? Was it pity? After deliberating for a minute, I don't think so. I saw the look in her eyes, and I didn't see any pity there.

When she grabbed my hand, I vividly remember the sparks. They were undeniable and unmistakable. Then, when I first saw her, like really saw her, she took my breath away. With her sitting there next to me, while Whitney was going off, all I could see was her.

Trying to shift and get a bit more comfortable, I'm hit with the unrelenting pain that has been constant, since I opened my eyes in the helicopter, and then passed back out again. Immediately, the memories of the accident begin going through my mind.

We never saw the IED, but it hit us hard. Moore's leg was under the debris, and I remember moving him, and the searing pain on my right side, and yelling for the guys. I remember pulling him with me, before a few of the other guys, who were behind us, came running over. As soon as they grabbed Moore, I guess I passed out. After that brief moment in the helicopter, I don't remember anything, but waking up here in this bed.

Then, a little later, I remember being so happy to see Whitney walking in. Even if my heart sank a little that she didn't look worried like Moore's family did when they got here. Whitney was all dolled up. Was that yesterday, or earlier today? Time seems to have no meaning. There don't seem to be any windows in the room, so I can't even tell if it's night or day.

I think back to Whitney's visit, and to have someone come for me. I was excited. I thought I'd be here alone. My parents couldn't afford to come or miss work. I know my mom must be freaking out right now.

Then, the words Whitney said crash back into me. I just couldn't believe it. Why did she even come? All that could have been said over the phone. My physical appearance was a deal breaker for her. I'm still the same person. I might have a few scars, but on the inside, I'm the same. But I never thought she was that type of girl to be so superficial.

Though, I guess I should have known. Whitney is a big social media personality and is always posting photos. Every chance she got, she'd get me to pose. It made her happy, so I did it, even if I wasn't a fan of having my photo taken all the time.

She was the first serious girlfriend I've had. I met her right after boot camp, and we had been dating for almost two years when I proposed. She had been hinting at it, and it felt like the right step. So, I popped the question, and then, I was shipping out a month later. We had been planning the wedding for when I got home from this deployment. Always picking out details in every letter or phone call, though I honestly could care less about flowers and colors, but I played the good groom to be.

My family didn't like her much, and my sisters said she was mean to them. I remember asking them to just try harder. Looking back, I should have put my sisters first. If I get the chance, I'm going to tell them how damn sorry I am.

When Whitney was around, my friends also started hanging out with me outside of work less and less, and eventually, just stopped. It should have been a red flag, but I just didn't see it.

I recalled looking over to Moore's bed, where his wife and sister were, so I didn't have to look at Whitney, as she talked. That's when I locked eyes with *her,* and the electricity in the room intensified. I can't describe it. It's not a feeling I had ever felt before. For a brief moment, I was pain free for the first time, since the blast.

Seeing the fire in her eyes, and how she looked at Whitney made my heart clench. Whitney's words hurt, but her breaking off the engagement didn't. I loved her, but I'm starting to realize I wasn't *in* love with her. I was in love with the idea of her. Of starting a family of my own, of having someone waiting on me back home, and someone to call and write to outside of my parents.

Whitney never made me feel the way I did when I looked at Moore's sister. When I think about her going after Whitney and hearing what she said to her, it took my breath away with how much passion was in her eyes. She put Whitney in her place and said everything I wish I could have.

When she came back, she came back to me.

*Me.*

I didn't tell her I wasn't heartbroken over Whitney, I couldn't talk at first. Not that talking, in general, is easy right now. My throat feels like sandpaper, and the effort to talk hurts all together.

Then, I remember what she said about the scars. I thought about that quote and realized right then that she was one of the people who didn't care about the scars. No one who believed those words would care. It makes me think she has some of her own she's hiding.

But the words she whispered right before I fell asleep, come back to me.

*'I'm not going anywhere. Fight for me and choose to live. I will be here when you wake up.'*

And she is. Right here, asleep on the edge of his bed. She kept her promise, and I knew right then I *would* fight. I would fight to see her every day for as long as she would visit me.

I'd fight for a chance to get to know her and to spend time with her. I'd fight to keep hearing her voice, to see her smile, and to hear her laugh.

Even though I know the chances are slim she'd want to be with me, once the bandages come off, I will fight for what time I can have with her. Some time is better than none at all. When I'm alone, I will have these memories to reach for, because I know most likely I'll be alone for the rest of my life.

I heard the doctors. I have bad burns on the entire right side of my body. From my head to my foot. Burns that will leave scars. Ugly scars that I won't be able to hide. Sure, I can wear long pants and long sleeves, and even gloves to hide my hand. Maybe, a turtleneck to hide my neck, but the ones on my face I won't be able to hide. Who's going to want to look at that every day? I already know I don't want, too.

I look down at her asleep and can't believe she stayed. She's resting her head on her arms, and her long, blonde hair is splayed out on the bed. The way the light catches her hair, it looks almost golden. I still can't believe she stayed.

I try to remember seeing her at our last homecoming. She had to be there, right? How do I not remember her? I know I was focused on Whitney, but someone who made me feel this way just by looking at them, I'd surely remember, right?

Whitney never made me feel this way, not once, not by looking at her, or when she touched me. It was just comfortable. Now, I don't think I can settle for comfortable again. I wonder how long these sparks will last. Maybe, it's just because this is all new, or maybe, it's the pain medication they have me on.

I think again of the sparks from when she grabbed my hand, and suddenly, I have to know if they are still there.

Very slowly, since everything still hurts, I move my hand to her head and gently run my hand through her hair. My hand tingles, so yes, the sparks are still there, which gets my heart racing. This gets the nurse's attention since the monitor near my bed starts going off.

They assume it's from the pain and come over to give me another dose of pain medication.

It's then I realize I don't know her name. I never paid much attention, when Moore talked about her, and most of the time, he would just refer to her as his sister.

Who was this beautiful girl, who stormed into my life? And what are the chances I can get her to stay?

# Chapter 3

**Lexi**

I wake up to hands, running through my hair. Without opening my eyes, I know it's Noah just by the sparks I feel. I could sit here and let him play with my hair forever, it's so calming. I don't want to move, and I don't want him to stop, because I want the sparks and whatever this is.

But even more than that, I need to know he's okay.

I open my eyes and sit up slowly. "You're awake," I say, smiling at him.

"You never… told me… your name." He says in a rough voice that's dry and scratchy from not being used. His words are slow and deliberate like it's hard for him to talk.

Reaching over, I get his water cup and bring the straw to his mouth. He takes a sip, before I set the cup back down.

"I'm Lexi," I say and squeeze his hand, needing the connection.

"Noah," he says his voice that sexy gritty baritone, even after the water. Maybe, that's just his voice. God, I hope so.

I smile at him, and I'm not able to see if he smiles or not, because of the bandages. Yet even so, his eyes seem to smile back at me. My heart clenches, and a cage of butterflies are released in my stomach. You'd think I never had a guy's attention on me before.

"I'm glad you decided to fight," I say truthfully and rub my thumb over the back of his hand.

"Well, when a... beautiful woman... asks me to fight... for her. How... could I not?" He says.

I feel my cheeks warm, and I sigh. "Such a flirt," I say, turning away from Noah for a minute to catch my breath.

Johnny is giving me a weird look, so I walk over and pull the curtain closed between their two beds.

"Mind your own business," I say to Johnny, and then watch his whole face break into a smile.

*Asshole.*

I glare at him before I sit back down, and Noah watches my every move.

"Guess I'll... get hell... for that later," Noah says with more of a smile in his voice than I have heard him with before. I know he's referring to Johnny being his Unit Leader.

"I can handle him, so you let me know if he gives you any trouble. Also, remind him of prom." I say louder to make sure Johnny hears.

When I hear Johnny yell, "You wouldn't dare!" I smirk and wink at Noah.

Smiling, I yell back, "Then mind your own business." I hear him grunt, but I know now he will at least try.

Noah tries to laugh, but then winces in pain, as he tries to shift.

"Want me to get a nurse to get you some more pain meds?"

"Yes," he says and takes a deep breath.

I walk over to the nurse's station, let them know, and then

head back to Noah.

He takes my hand. "Talk to me, until they get here."

Just then, the doctor comes in to talk to him. I squeeze his hand, "I'll leave and let you two talk."

"No, stay," he says, his eyes pleading.

I nod and sit back down. The doctor looks surprised.

"To be honest, I'm surprised you're even awake. Normally, the body will shut down to heal." The doctor goes on. "But if you're talking, it's a good sign. We didn't have to put you in a medically induced coma, as you have mostly second degree burns with some third degree burns. They won't heal pretty, and we think you will need some skin grafts, but won't know for sure, until the healing is further along. Though, we will monitor you for signs of infection in the burns, as they heal. We will need to do one graft here for sure, and maybe, more to get you stable for the trip home. Once you are stateside, you can be seen by a plastic surgeon to minimize scarring."

It's a lot to take in, but as bad as it is he still sounds like he was extremely lucky.

"Internally, you have had a significant amount of bleeding, so we need to make sure all your organs are working, before we move you stateside as well." The doctor continues, "So far, everything looks good, but we aren't out of the woods yet. But with enough rest and physical therapy, I believe you'll recover fully." I nod and squeeze Noah's hand, and the doctor continues.

"Once you're healed, you will need physical therapy on your right leg and right arm, since the muscles were injured pretty badly. However, if you do as the therapist says, you will regain up to 95% control with them again, and there's a good chance you will recover 100%."

"Though, when you are stateside, you will be required to see a therapist and psychologist. I know the last thing you want to do is talk about it, but I have seen where patients who talk and work through it actually physically heal faster. So, I encourage it."

"Any questions for me?" The doctor asks.

"How long, before he can go stateside?" I ask.

"That depends on Noah, and how long, before he's stable. We can't move him until then, and also until the risk of infection is gone. It's too long of a flight. Could be a few weeks, or it could be a month."

I nod, and then look at Noah.

"Any other questions?" I ask him.

"No." He says.

"I'll send a nurse over with some pain medicine," he says, walking over to Johnny's bed.

Becky pulls the curtain away and holds her hand out for me. A silent ask for support. That's why I'm here, so I squeeze Noah's hand and walk over to stand beside Becky. She wraps an arm around my shoulders, and I wrap one around her waist and hold her as tight as I can.

This is the first time we will have talked to a doctor, and while we have assumed he's okay, because he's up and talking, we have no idea. I need to remember as much as possible because I know my mom will ask a million questions.

When I see the doctor looks confused why I'm over at this bed as well, I smile saying, "That's my brother."

The doctor shrugs and talks to Johnny, "As you know, you lost part of your leg below the knee in the blast. We've been keeping an eye on it, but I think the time for infection on it has almost passed, and also on your other wounds. When you

17

came in, you had a collapsed lung and some internal injuries, which we are still monitoring. Before we send you stateside, we want to make sure everything is working properly."

"No way. I stay until the last man from my unit goes back," Johnny says.

I'm hit with pride for him. He's always been protective of me and of Becky, but seeing how he is with his men, is a whole new level.

"I figured you would say that based on your file. We expect the last one to travel will be Mr. Carr here, which is why we placed you two next to each other."

Johnny nods. "I'm not leaving his side," he says to the doctor.

The doctor smiles and makes a note on his chart.

"How are the rest of the guys?" Johnny asks hesitantly.

"Doing well. Donell should be heading home in a few days, and Avery isn't far behind him. The others will be a bit longer, but everyone is stable." The doctor says, staring at Johnny. They seem to have a silent conversation before Johnny gives the man a firm nod and moves to the next bed.

That's when it hits me what Johnny was asking silently. He wanted to know if anyone else had died and if everyone else would live.

"Johnny," I say and turn to him. "How many guys did you lose?"

Johnny cringes. "One in the field, and one on the way here."

Almost on autopilot, I'm at his side and hugging him. After a minute, he grips me back just as tight.

"It's not your fault. Those families will not blame you." I whisper to him.

"It still feels like my fault. I should have saved them." He says, taking a shaky breath.

"I know." Is all I can say.

Becky rubs my back, as Johnny and I stay locked in our hug a moment more. We have always been close, and his marrying my best friend only brought us closer.

When I stand, I turn to face my best friend, and she hugs me without a word, before closing the curtain again.

I go back to Noah's bed, and he watches my every move.

"The nurse bring you pain medicine yet?" I ask.

"No." He says.

"You rest. I'll talk until the nurse gets here. What do you want me to talk about?" I ask Noah.

"You," he says.

So, I start telling him about what being Johnny's sister is like and some stories from our childhood, like when Johnny put a frog in my bed, and how much trouble he got in. The nurse comes over, and it's not long into the next story of our tree house that he drifts off to sleep.

I walk over to Becky and see Johnny is asleep, too.

"Want to head out and get a shower and some clean clothes, before they wake up?" I ask her.

She nods.

"We shouldn't be more than an hour. We can grab some food from the hotel restaurant, too." I say, wrapping my arm through Becky's, as we leave.

With the hotel being across from the hospital, it makes things really easy. While she showers, I'll get some food and coffee. Then, she'll eat, while I take one of the quickest showers of all time, and I'll eat on the way back to the guys.

Becky stops on the sidewalk in front of the hospital.

"Listen, I want to say this without Johnny around. We all watched what you have been through, and we want you happy.

19

I'm beyond thrilled with the way you handled Whitney. Hell, I'd have backed you up, if you had punched the twit in her face. She's horrible. Just be careful is all I'm going to say."

"Becky…" I start.

"No, that's all I'm going to say. You and your brother, that playfulness is back between you two, and it's been missing since… well, you know. You smiled today, and you don't smile much anymore. If you're happy, then I'll handle Johnny, okay?"

Her words have so much more meaning than what she actually said. I get a bit choked up and just nod. What can you say, when your best friend reminds you once again, she has your back, even if it puts you between her and her husband, who happens to be your brother?

# Chapter 4

**Noah**

I wake up and have to blink a few times to let my eyes adjust to the light. Everything still hurts, and even my hair hurts. Is that even possible? I lay there for a minute, before opening my eyes again.

*Lexi.*

God, she's beautiful, and she makes me forget why I'm in this bed, even if it's for a little bit. It's only been a few days, but I can't picture my life without her in it.

She makes everything better. She's my reason to fight.

To fight to live. To fight for me. To fight for her.

I *will* fight for her.

I finally open my eyes, and it takes a moment to focus, but I don't see Lexi.

I groan.

*Idiot.*

Of course, she left, because she doesn't want a crippled monster. What was I thinking? Not that I can blame her. A girl like that has to have guys lining up to be with her. She can have her pick of anyone she wants, and she doesn't want me. I need to remember that.

As soon as I finish that thought, I hear her voice, coming through the door. I see her with Moore's wife, and they both have coffee in their hand and new clothes on.

When she sees me, her smile lights up the room. Then, she sits down next to me, and I can't help but sigh in relief. At least, I won't be in the hospital alone.

"I thought… you left," I say.

She sets her coffee down and squeezes my hand, and then lifts the straw to my mouth.

"No, I just needed a shower, a change of clothes, and coffee." She says.

"I don't really… want to be alone… here." He says.

"I wouldn't want to be alone either." She says, taking my hand.

"What's all that?" I ask when I notice she has a bag with her, and she pulls out a tablet.

"So, what do you want me to talk about this time, or would you rather me grab a book to read you?" She asks, holding up the tablet.

"Tell me about you. How long… can you stay? I'm sure you have… to get back to work." I say.

She beams a smile at me, and I realize I'm addicted to that smile. I *need* more of them. I wish I knew what makes her smile because I'd do more of it.

"I'm my own boss actually," she says while pulling out her laptop.

"I can do everything I need to right here," she places a hand on her computer. "I'm here as long as my brother is, and since he's staying until you're ready to go back, then it looks like you're stuck with me."

22

If I could smile, I think I'd smile so big it'd filled my whole face right now. She's staying, even if it isn't for me, she's staying. It's a relief.

"Tell me about… work," I say, and then listen to her explain that she's a social media guru and food blogger. She helps manage some blogs and small businesses social media accounts, but she had cut back on that because she prefers to write.

"I also run an online food website with recipes and cooking tips, product reviews, and such. I put out an online magazine as well and am working on publishing a cookbook." She says.

Shrugging, she continues, "The Wi-Fi here at the hospital has a decent connection, and that's all I need to work. I have enough recipes on backlog with photos to edit and write up. I can mix that with posts on the website, and I should be fine. Worst case, I have a friend that has done some recipe shoots for me before that I can reach out, to. I also have a few videos I've been working on editing. So, I have plenty to keep me busy."

"She's an amazing cook. The cookies in the care packages I get. Those were made by her." Moore interjects from the bed next to me.

I remember those care packages. I'd get a bit jealous because it seemed each time we got mail he had care packages from his parents, his wife, or his sister. The Unit waited for the ones from his sister because they were always filled with cookies and baked treats.

I was lucky if my parents were able to send one care package per deployment. Money was always so tight with them. They have put all their extra money into taking care of my grandpa, my dad's dad. He's the only living grandparent I have. He has Alzheimer's and has to be in a special nursing home with all sorts of locks and safety measures.

It's not cheap, and he's been there for five years now. My parents never complain, but being the oldest, I've always felt I needed to help out. I got a job after school the moment I could. My parents refused to take money from me to help with the bills, so I took the money I made and made sure my sisters had clothes and school supplies, bought Christmas and birthday presents, and added groceries to our pantry each month.

There was no money for college, and let's be honest, I didn't have the grades, so I joined the Marines. Then, I started sending money home each month. It took me a bit to convince my parents I was okay. Since I stayed in the barracks, the only expenses I had were my phone and car.

Though, I'm guessing now, I'll be discharged and need to figure something else out. My heart starts to race thinking about it. The money is directly deposited from my paycheck into my parent's bank account, but am I still getting a paycheck?

My heart monitor starts beeping, as my mind races, but I'm pulled from it, when Lexi takes my hand.

"Hey. It's okay. You're safe, and I'm right here. Look at me." She says in a calming voice.

I turn my head enough that I can focus on her.

"There you are." She smiles, and the heart monitor slows. "You got too far in your own head there. I know it's easier said than done, but you need to stop that. Want me to keep talking?" She asks.

"Yes," I say.

"Well, Johnny is right. I love to cook, but it's hard for just one, so I don't cook as much as I'd like. The cookbook is more of a hobby for me. I always thought it would be cool to do a cookbook, so I'm going to finish one and sell it on my website.

24

Becky has been my taste tester with Johnny gone, and now my dad since he's stuck at home, after his back surgery."

That explains why her parents aren't here. When I shift and cringe in pain, she stands up to get the nurse for some pain medication.

"You go to sleep. I'm going to get some work done and will be here when you wake up, okay?"

I just nod, and the last thing I remember, before falling asleep is how she looks like an angel the way the light is hitting her hair.

# Chapter 5

**Lexi**

We fall into a good routine. Noah has had one skin graft, and the doctors say they will do more, once he gets stateside. Because the doctors keep Noah out with the pain medicine most of the day, we only get about fifteen to thirty minutes every eight hours to talk, and I give him my full attention.

At first, it was me talking and him listening, but the last few days, he's been talking to me more and opening up. He's told me about his family and joining the military. Talking is still a bit hard, but the more he speaks, the easier it seems to get.

When he sleeps, I either nap, work, or slip out to the hotel room for a shower. While I'm at the hotel, I make it a point to call Mom and Dad each day with updates. They demand video calls because they want to see me themselves and make sure I'm taking care of myself. Since we can't have our phone on in the hospital, I've made a few videos with my tablet and have been able to send them regularly.

Now that Johnny is doing well, my parents have focused on how Noah is doing. When I told them we wouldn't be home as soon as planned, because Johnny refused to leave Noah's side, I saw pride on my parent's faces. They hate that Noah doesn't have anyone.

I guess, Becky told them about my encounter with Whitney, because my mom asked why I didn't give her a black eye, and my dad was proud I showed restraint. I can't win with those two.

I've had a few calls from Becky's parents, too. They want to check on me, but also want to know that Becky is okay and taking care of herself. They're worried, and I can't blame them.

Becky and I worked it out, so one of us is here at all times. I didn't want Noah waking up again and feeling like I might have left him.

It broke my heart when he said that he thought I had left. It was never my intention for him to feel alone. It's hard for him to talk, and I know he's disoriented from being asleep all the time. I wanted to offer him something solid to hold on to.

We have been here just shy of three weeks now, and I have to say, if it weren't for being in a hospital, I would like the routine we have set up.

When I notice Noah starting to wake up, I save my work and close my laptop. Then, I reach over and take his hand.

"Hey, good morning," I say to him. I started doing this to orient him on the time of day it was since there are no windows to look out nor are there any clocks he can see.

Johnny is in his bed reading a book, but I can feel his eyes on me. He has been watching me these few weeks. Though, he hasn't said anything, he keeps an eye on me. Becky said Johnny's happy I've been helping Noah, and he hates to think he'd be alone without us. But the way he watches me, I can see his wheels turning.

"Hey," Noah says, his voice dry and scratchy.

I grab his water and lift the straw to his mouth. He takes a sip, then I ask, "Are you hungry?" He nods.

He's moving his head more now, and when they changed out his bandages, I can see his mouth.

They have him on a liquid meal shake, so he can use a straw. I go grab one from the nurse's station fridge and bring it up to his mouth. He forces down a few sips with a grimace.

"I know they're gross, huh?" I ask him.

"Yeah," he says and takes a few more sips.

"Well, once you're cleared for real food, I'll make you a home cooked meal, anything you want," I say to Noah.

"Hey, brother here. What about me? I can eat real food!" Johnny whines.

"You also haven't been forced to drink these shakes for weeks. Trust me, I tried one, and they're gross. Remember that cough medicine Grandma would give us any time we were sick? It's worse than that. He deserves a year of home cooked food." I tell Johnny.

Our grandma thought this cough medicine could cure anything. I'm pretty sure she made it herself. There was never a label on it, and it tasted horrible like dirt, curdled milk, and vinegar.

Johnny's face goes serious for a moment, and he gets this calculating look in his eye, but it's gone just as fast, and he's back to my playful big brother.

"Keep it up, and I'll tell Mom, and she'll demand you come over for dinner more often," Johnny says.

"Don't you dare," I say.

"Oh, I dare." He fires back.

We lock eyes and stare each other down until the doctor

comes in.

While they check Noah's bandages, I step outside the curtain. I want to see under them so badly, but I know he isn't ready for that, and I won't push him.

When the doctor comes out, he looks at Noah and Johnny. "Well, looks like you two are going home. Where do you want to be transferred?"

"Camp Clarke," Johnny says.

Camp Clarke is in southern Georgia. When Johnny and Becky were married, they found a place halfway between the base and her school in Savannah, and each of them only had about a twenty-minute drive. We were lucky he was stationed there, since we live right outside Savannah, Georgia.

Then Noah says. "I don't have anyone, and my parents can't take time off to help me, and there's no base near them."

I grab his hand. "Come back to Camp Clarke with us."

He looks at me for a minute "You live near there?"

"Yes, I live in Clark Springs," I say.

He pauses to think for a minute, and I find myself holding my breath. I want him to come back with us more than I realize. Though, I can go anywhere he is if he doesn't choose to come back with me. I feel like he would be choosing to get away from me, but I will have plenty of time on the plane home to sort out these crazy feelings.

"That's where I'll go, then," he says.

"Okay, I'll get the orders going. You ladies will have to make your own plans because you can't ride with them." The doctor looks at us, and we nod.

"Doc," Noah says. "Can we get Lexi on the forms so she can see me when we get there?"

When he says that, I smile. He wants me there, and that

means everything to me. Knowing I'm helping him and will have more time with him, is a relief.

"Of course, I'll take care of it. She's special this one." The doctor smiles at me. "We will let you know, but they'll be heading out sometime tomorrow."

I look over at Noah after the doctor leaves and smile at him. "Don't you dare stop fighting, when you're on that plane. I'll be waiting for you at the other end." I say.

"Promise?" He asks.

"I promise," I say, squeezing his hand.

The nurse comes over to start prepping both of them, and before Becky and I go, I lean over and kiss Noah's hand.

"See you stateside, Soldier," I say, before I head back to the hotel.

Becky and I book our flight and call to let Mom and Dad know we're coming home.

That night as I lay in bed, I can't help but think this is the first night I've spent away from Noah, since we met, and I don't like it one bit.

# Chapter 6

**Noah**

They're getting ready to load Moore and me and transport us to the plane.

"Hey, we're going to give you something to knock you out, because the transportation from the hospital to the plane is bumpy. The doctor thinks it's best if you are out for it." The nurse says.

"Okay. How is the plane ride?" I ask.

"A lot like your plane ride there. Smooth, unless you hit turbulence. They have medicine to knock you out if it gets too bad."

I nod, when another nurse comes up with a big smile on her face.

Grinning, she says, "You have a call."

Thankfully, she holds the phone for me to my good ear.

"Hello?"

"Hey, it's Lexi." Her warm voice comes over the line, and even though it hurts, I still smile. "I got used to being there when you get up each morning, so I was hoping to catch you before they boarded you. We have another hour, before our

31

flight. Just wanted you to know I was thinking about you."

My heart races, and the stupid heart rate monitor tells the room. This causes both nurses to smile at me.

"I was thinking about you too, and I'll see you soon," I say, wishing I could talk more to her.

"Yes, you will. See you soon, Noah." She says as we say our goodbyes.

The nurse with the phone winks at me, "That was a totally illegal phone call, so it didn't happen."

"What didn't happen?" I ask.

She nods and walks away. The first nurse smiles at me with a syringe of medicine in her hand. "Ready?"

"I'm ready to go see her, yes."

\* \* \*

I wake up later on, and I'm still on the plane. Moore is next to me, and we have a nurse at our bedside. There are two doctors walking past the beds, and four other beds of soldiers, being transferred as well.

I stare at the metal of the plane roof and think of Lexi. She has spent the last few weeks with me only leaving, when she had to, and mostly to shower and change clothes.

I hated she was there having to take care of me, and as much as I didn't like it, I couldn't force her to leave. The only reassurance I have is that she could have chosen to walk away at any point and claimed work or family, and she didn't.

She says we're friends, and this is what friends do.

I can't help but smile. I was never good with girls. Hell,

Whitney was my only relationship, and the only girl I've ever kissed, and my first at just about everything. She was comfortable.

But Lexi, she makes my heart race and takes my breath away. Before this accident, I'd have pursued her and not thought twice, but now, I know how I'm going to come out of this.

It's not going to be pretty, and Lexi deserves so much more, I want to give her the world. She deserves to go out and live in it, and not hidden away with someone who will scare people every time they go out. I have her as a friend, and I won't let go of that until she makes me. It will be enough.

It has to be enough.

I'll have her any way I can, I don't dare dream she might be mine someday. I'm sure a girl like her wants kids. Though, I didn't tell her, but one of the times the doctor came in while she was gone, he said they didn't know the extent of the damage down there. Basically, they don't know, if I'll ever be able to get it up again or get hard, much less have kids.

So, friends we will stay.

I look over at the nurse.

"Want some more pain medicine?" She asks. I just nod, and in just a few minutes, I'm drifting off again.

\* \* \*

When I wake up, I'm in a hospital room, and I see Lexi with her back to me, looking out the window. My throat is dry, and I ache all over, but I can't stop watching her. She's in shorts, flip flops, and an old worn out t-shirt. By the looks of it, she wears it a lot. Her blonde hair is thrown up in a messy bun, and she looks comfortable.

"Lexi," I say, but I don't recognize my own voice, because it's dry and scratchy.

She turns around, and I see shock, and then relief crosses her face, as she rushes to my side.

"Noah, thank God!" She says, rushing over and grabbing my hand. Then, she gets the water from the side table and holds the straw to my mouth. The water feels good on my throat, and I study her, as a take a few slow sips.

She looks so damn beautiful that it makes my chest hurt, but I can tell something is wrong. It looks like she was crying. The thought of her crying guts me, and that's when I know I'm in deep with this girl.

I remember my dad always saying he couldn't take my mom's tears, because it would wound him. I remember one night when my grandmother died, and my mom was crying uncontrollably into my dad's shoulder, and I saw tears, running down his face.

When I asked him about it later, he said yes, he was sad my grandmother had died, but it hurt worse that my mom was crying, and he couldn't stop it. He said he'd do anything to take away her pain. I was thirteen at the time, and I remember thinking I want a love like that someday.

Looking at Lexi now, the thought of her crying, well, I'm starting to understand how my dad felt that night.

I take one more sip of water. "What's wrong?" I ask her. If I know what has her upset, I might be able to fix it, or at least, comfort her.

She takes a deep breath "The plane ride was pretty rough. I guess, they hit some weather and decided to keep you under, but you reacted weirdly to the medication they gave you. They expected you to wake up three days ago. The doctor kept saying it was your body's way of healing, but it didn't make it any easier not to know when or…if you would wake up."

I let that sink in. I've been out for almost four days now, but the next thought I have is she was upset, because of me.

*Me.*

This strange feeling washes over me, and I can't explain it. In that moment, the pain is gone, the memories of the explosion gone, and the worry of the fight ahead gone.

In that moment, all I see is this beautiful girl worried about me. Somehow in the back of my mind, I know as long as she's here, everything will be okay.

"That explains how I feel," I say. My whole body is stiff and sore, and I feel about as bad as I did when I woke up on the way to Germany. Worry crosses her face, as she presses the call button for the nurse.

"Have you been here the whole time?" I ask.

"Yes, but they kick me out after visiting hours." She says and then is a softer voice, "I was so worried you would wake up, when I wasn't here. I didn't want you to be alone."

My damn heart starts beating faster than a racehorse at the Kentucky Derby. I want her words to mean so much more, but I know we're just friends. I remind myself I'm in the friend zone, and that's it.

The nurse comes in and sees I'm awake. She checks the monitors and says, "I'll go get the doctor. See, Lexi, we told you he was okay." She places a hand on Lexi's shoulder, before walking out the door.

"You even had the staff worried about you?" I ask.

"Oh, that's your nurse, Brooke. She's been really great and

comes in and just talks with me, so I wasn't sitting in here alone. We've bonded, and I figured we should since you'll be here a while."

Lexi sits down beside my bed and takes my unscarred hand in both of hers. The warmth that shoots through my arm from her touch is calming. She leans over and rests her forehead on my hand, while she's still holding it.

I feel her take a deep breath, and then a minute later she says, "Don't you dare scare me like that again. Do you hear me?" She looks up and locks eyes with mine.

In her stormy eyes, I see the concern and the worry from the last three days, but there's something more hidden in them.

Something I'm too broken to hope for.

# Chapter 7

**Lexi**

Three days.

The doctors said he would wake up any time when he got to his room. After the first forty-eight hours, I knew they were worried, and at least, one nurse, Brooke, was honest with me and said it's not good that he hadn't. She explained what the doctors didn't and that it was most likely his body, shutting down to heal.

She has been my rock through it all, making sure I ate and sneaking me in the good food from the nurse's area. Becky and Johnny are on a different floor now, so it's harder for her to watch me and me to watch her, but each night, she checks in on me.

Three days of not seeing his eyes almost broke me. Crazy, right? It's been about three weeks, and he's been out sleeping a lot of that time, but there's something here, and I feel it.

There are sparks and a connection I can't deny, no matter how hard I try. When I let my mind wander to the thought that he might not wake up, it killed me. It also destroyed me every time I had to walk out that door because visiting hours were over. Stupid visiting hours.

I look up at Noah and see him watching me.

"I promise to always fight my way back to you." He says, squeezing my hand, and it's the best I can hope for.

The doctor comes in and checks him over and asks him some questions, before giving the nurse a few orders. As the last few days toss round in my head, I block it all out. My parents have been by every day. They spend some time with Johnny, and then they come to keep me company. But it was still hard for my dad to be here for long periods of time, so while their visits were short, and they have been a nice distraction.

Thankfully, the doctor interrupts my thoughts and pulls me back to the present. "Tomorrow, we're going to change your bandages. I want to see them for myself, and how they're healing. Though, it will likely be painful, we can't give you any extra pain medicine, because I need to assess which ones are still causing pain. With your medication schedule, we'll do this at eleven in the morning, as your morning dose wears off." He says.

Noah looks at me and says, "As long as she's here."

Be still my heart, as my grandma used to say. Who wouldn't want a guy to need you and want you like that?

I nod. "I'll be here," I reassure him.

Once they leave, I help him with another one of the meal shakes.

"These shakes taste a fraction of a bit better than the ones in Germany." He says.

"Whatever meal you want. I mean it." I remind him, which earns me a bit of a smile.

"How's Johnny?" He asks.

"Ready to start physical therapy. I guess, he can't wait to get out of the hospital, as I'm sure you can't either. He's in good spirits according to Becky, but I haven't seen him but for a minute, since you guys got here." I tell him.

I help him find something on TV to watch, all the while, we're constantly touching each other, holding hands, my hand on his arm, or his hand on mine. For me, it's a reminder that he's awake, and he's fine. I like to think he needs to reassure himself that I'm here, but I doubt that's the case.

Before I know it, Becky peeks her head in.

"Hey, girl. They're getting ready to kick us out."

"You're leaving?" He asks me.

"Yeah, they make me leave, when visiting hours are over, but I'll be back tomorrow. I plan to go see Johnny first, and then, I'll be here. Twenty minutes tops." I say.

He nods, as worry crosses his face. We really haven't been apart, and this will be his first night alone. That he will remember anyway.

I look at Becky, "Give us a minute?" She nods and heads out to the hallway.

I walk over to Noah and take his hand in mine. I lean down to look him in the eye. "Hey, the nurse is going to give you some sleeping medicine, and I doubt you'll even know I'm gone. But I *will* see you tomorrow, okay?"

He takes a deep breath, "Okay." He says, and then like clockwork, the nurse comes in with his medicine. She injects it into his IV, and I stay just a moment and watch his eyes get heavy.

"Get some sleep, Soldier." I smile and give his hand a squeeze.

I walk out with Becky like I do every night. "Good to see him awake." She says with a knowing smile on her face.

"Yeah, it is," I say.

She turns in the elevator and looks at me. "You like him, don't you?"

"Well, yes, we're friends," I say, trying to play it off like it's nothing.

"No, you like him, like him."

I shake my head. "He's in no condition to start a relationship."

"That not what I asked." She pins me with one of her *I'm your best friend so stop bull shitting me*' stares.

"Yes, I like him. Okay?" I look at her, and she waits for me to continue. "There's a connection, but again, this is no time to start anything. Plus, I have nothing left to give."

"You have to live again sometime." She says with that sadness I have come to know and hate in her voice.

"I am living, it's just not how everyone wants me to, but it's how I want to, and I'd appreciate it, if you all let me be," I say and walk away from her to my car, thankful she doesn't follow me and push the subject.

On the drive home, I think of my conversation with Becky. I was harsh, but I know she'll act like it never happened. That's what she does. She pushes me when I don't even realize I need it, but she knows I need it.

I guess, that's why we have been best friends, since Kindergarten. She was the new girl in class a few months into the school year. That day I was wearing my *Beauty and the Beast* Disney princess shirt, and she had on a *Cinderella* one.

She was sitting alone, so I sat down next to her and shared my dislike for Disney's *Lion King*, and she agreed. She laughed at the story of my brother, watching it over and over again, and then singing the songs at the top of his lungs to drive me crazy. We have been friends ever since.

About the time we reached middle school, she was over at my

house all the time. Then, her parents started traveling more. She tried to pass it off as traveling for work, but we knew it wasn't. So, my parents made the guest room hers, and she'd stay with us at least half of every month. I loved it because she was the sister I always wanted.

Her parents weren't bad people they just focused on their lives and treated Becky as an equal, and not their child. My parents treated her as their daughter and pretty much raised her. When Johnny left to go to boot camp, I could tell the two of them had something, but they were fighting it. I suspected it was out of some loyalty to me. I approved and pushed them together.

They had a bumpy road but worked it out, and the day they got married, and she legally became my sister, was one of the happiest days of my life. She's the one who tells me things and doesn't care if it's not what I want to hear. She doesn't walk on eggshells around me. I need that more than I will ever admit.

My thoughts turn to Noah. I hate leaving him at night. The thought of him alone there kills me. It's been a long time since I've cared this much about anyone that isn't family. But I meant what I said to Becky, I don't have anything left to give to anyone.

Pulling into my driveway, my dream house comes into view. The dream house I've wanted since I was a kid.

You would think all my dreams had come true. You'd be wrong.

# Chapter 8

### Lexi

The next day I go see Johnny first thing, just like I said I would. He's in good spirits, and I guess Becky has a lot to do with that. She isn't here yet, so I get Johnny to myself for a bit.

"I talked to Becky last night," he tells me. "Is it true you like Noah?"

I turn my back to him because I can't look at him and have this conversation. "Yes, but I have no plans of telling him," I say.

"He's one of the good guys, Lexi. He's the best guy in my unit, and he got dealt a shit hand because he chose to save me."

Neither of us says anything. We all know we owe Noah so much more than we could ever hope to repay him.

"I asked him about it you know, saving me," Johnny continues. "You know what his answer was?"

I turn around now and look at him and shake my head no.

"He said I had something to live for. I reminded him about Whitney, and he said in his gut he knew she wasn't the one."

Looking away, I walk to the window staring out, my back to Johnny, but he keeps talking.

"He sends money home every month to help his family, and he'd give you the shirt off his back. I didn't think you'd ever go for another military guy, but if I could pick anyone for you, it would be Noah."

My heart clenches. He's talking about my husband. My dead husband, who wasn't lucky enough to live through the IED blast. He didn't make it home.

After a minute, Johnny speaks again. "Come here, Lex," he says softly.

I turn to look at him, and he pats the bed next to him. I walk over and sit down next to him. He wraps his arms around me, hugging me to him, and I rest my head on his shoulder, and we talk just like old times. When I was younger, and I'd get scared, we'd sit just like this. Then, he'd tell stories of what was going on in school, or about his friends, until I'd fall asleep. Then, he'd carry me back to bed.

Right now, he's telling me about Mom coming to visit and fussing over him and asking why I haven't been home, and why I'm spending so much time with someone other than him. Though, he reassured me that he covered for me by telling her about Noah, and how he didn't have anyone, so he asked me to be there for him, and how Mom said she was proud of me.

Before I know it, he has me laughing, recounting how Mom has been fussing over him nonstop. I'm laughing when Becky comes in.

"This right here warms my heart. But girl, you are in my spot." She laughs.

"He's all yours," I say, and then I notice I've been here almost an hour already. "Well, I need to go see Noah. I'm late," I tell them.

I say goodbye and then go to Noah's room. His nurse,

Brooke, is coming out of his room, and she smiles when she sees me.

"He doesn't think you're coming today." She says to me.

"Oh, I went to visit my brother first, and we got caught up talking. He's here, too."

She nods, "You have been very good for him, but he needs to keep pushing. He's slowly coming out of the pain medicine, so we can check his bandages. Let me know if you need anything."

"Thank you, Brooke." I hug her.

"You're welcome, Lexi." She says, moving off to her next patient.

I stand in front of Noah's room and take a deep breath. I knock on his door and peek my head inside. His eyes are closed, so I walk over and take his hand, thinking he's asleep and not wanting to wake him, but needing to let him know I'm here.

He squeezes my hand and slowly opens his eyes. I can see the pain in them, and it breaks my heart.

"You came," he whispers.

"Of course, I did. I'm sorry I'm late. Johnny and I got to talking, and when I looked up, I couldn't believe what time it was. It's always been like that with us. I should have set an alarm."

He lightly squeezes my hand. "No, he's your brother, and you need to see him, too." He whispers.

I smile at him and can tell he's fighting the pain, and also looking like he wants to go to sleep. "I'm not going anywhere, so get some rest."

He closes his eyes, so I pull out my computer to get some work done. A few hours later Brooke comes in and asks me to call her in when he's awake.

I get in another hour of work before he starts to wake up. I close my computer and take his hand. He opens his eyes, and they lock on mine. Neither of us says a word, but so much passes between us. While our eyes are locked, there's a buzz in the air, and it's like everything stands still and time stops.

The spell is broken, when my phone pings, letting me know I have a text message. Ignoring it, I press the nurse call button. Brooke pokes her head in and smiles, "Let me get the doctor."

The doctor comes in and says he wants to be here when they change Noah's bandages to see for himself how he's healing and determine their next moves.

I smile at Noah, "I'll go for a walk."

He tightens his hold on my hand, "Please, stay." There's a hint of panic in his voice. Knowing I need to at least be out of the way, I look to the other side of the room.

"I'll go sit on the couch over there, okay?"

He nods.

The nurse closes the curtain, and they start with his leg. I'm listening to them, saying his leg is healing nicely with the exception of a few spots. When they begin working on the arm bandages, I can hear his cry of pain.

"Lexi." He groans.

"I'm right here, Noah."

"Come here, please." He says desperately.

Brooke pokes her head out of the curtain and nods at me. I take the chair on his left side and hold his hand.

I see the pain in his eyes when he looks at me.

"You don't have to watch, but I need you." His voice breaks me. I haven't been needed like this in so long.

"Sweet, Noah," I sigh. "Blood doesn't scare me. I've seen a lot worse."

After my husband passed, I volunteered with injured soldiers who were recuperating. My husband didn't make it home, but these guys did. Some of the wounds were pretty gruesome, especially when they would push too hard and reopen them.

"Distract me," he begs.

I don't even think, as I just start talking.

"So, I had this dream growing up that I'd own one of those old southern plantations. You know the ones with the long oak tree lined driveways and the huge front porches? The ones built, before the Civil War. I loved driving by them and watched many being restored, but so many others still need some love."

While the doctor and Brooke work, he never takes his eyes off me, so I keep talking.

"Well after," I pause, closing my eyes, and taking a deep breath. He encourages me, squeezing my hand. "After, I went looking and found one. It was perfect. It has fifty acres, trees lining a long driveway, and even has a lake in the back with a willow tree, but it needed some love."

He flinches, so I squeeze his hand and start rubbing it with my thumb and keep talking. "The lady who owned it was selling it and had been in her family, since right after the Civil War, but she had no one to leave it, too. She had outlived her kids, and she was an only child, so she put it on the market. I bought it, Noah."

I pause, watching his eyes go big. "Everyone told me I was crazy with this huge house and me there all by myself, but I didn't care." I glance over and see some of the burns on his ribs, and they look pretty good compared to some others I've seen before. I notice the doctor seems pleased.

Then, I take a deep breath and smile at Noah, who is

watching me watch the doctor.

"So, the first thing I did, when I got the keys was take before photos of the grounds, both inside and outside the house. I wanted to be able to show people how far it had come. That first year I stood at the end of the driveway and took a photo, looking up the tree lined drive towards the house. Then, I took another one in spring with the flowers in bloom, one on a bright sunny day in summer with all the green colors, one in the fall with the leaves changing with the vibrant red and orange colors, and finally, one in winter with it all glistening white and snow covered."

I smile thinking about it, "I have those photos framed and hung them along the stair wall, so everyone can see them. The house is pretty big. There are two main areas, the first and the second floors, but the attic is done up. With a few adjustments, you could get two or three bedrooms up there. There are five bedrooms on the second floor. The master bedroom is on the first floor, which is nice because it keeps me living mostly on one floor. The basement is finished thank God, because unfinished basements creep me out. It's set up like an apartment down there with a kitchen area and two more bedrooms. There's also a laundry room and lots of storage, too."

The nurse shifts him to his side, facing me a bit, as they work on the bandages on his shoulder.

"The dining room on the main floor is huge, and it could fit a twenty-person table easily. I set it up as my photo area, where I take photos and have my backdrops and lighting. There are several fireplaces around the house. They were the first things I fixed up when I moved in. I wanted to keep them and be able to use them. I love curling up with a good book by the fireplace in the winter."

I smile and look over at Brooke again. She nods her head for me to keep going.

"I'm also pretty sure one of the storage rooms in the basement was one part of The Underground Railroad. I want to bring someone to take a look, but Johnny made a good point. If I bring someone in now, and they say yes and mark the house as a historical location, then I have to follow all sorts of guidelines in restoring the property. There would be a lot of hoops to jump through. So, I'll wait, until I'm done restoring it and plan to leave that section untouched. There are a bunch of old boxes down there too, but I haven't touched them just in case."

I see a small smile in Noah's eyes, and then we hear the doctor. "Okay, this is the worst part. We need to do his neck and face."

Noah's hand grips mine tighter, and I can see the panic in his eyes.

"Wait, hang on," I tell them, and the doctor nods, as he saw Noah's face, too.

I turn and look into Noah's eyes. "What's wrong?" I ask him.

His eyes plead with me and whispers, "I want you to keep talking, but..." He trails off.

"But what?" I ask gently. He keeps looking into my eyes never breaking the connection.

"Noah, you can tell me anything, you know that, right?"

He takes a deep breath "I don't think I'm ready for you to see the scars there, and I know I'm not ready to see them."

I nod. "Then I won't," I say and shift the chair around. I hold his hand in both of mine and place my forehead on top of his hand, so I'm now looking at the floor.

"How's this?" I ask.

"Perfect." He says barely above a whisper.

I hear the doctor and Brooke moving around again.

"So, is the chimney the only thing you have restored?" Brooke asks me to get the conversation rolling again.

I smile. "I had the hardwood floors restored throughout the house on the first and second floor. Some were pretty bad, but I had a guy come in, and he was able to match the floor, where it needed to be replaced. Once it was sanded down and stained again, you can't tell the difference between the old and the new. I had someone come in and check the water pipes and electricity to make sure they were up to code. Oh, and the first year I added an HVAC unit because I had to have air conditioning. Otherwise, I would have died in that house in the summer. I had the air set up, so each floor has its own unit since I don't use the basement or the second floor when it's just me there. The electric bills still make me cringe each month."

"So, it's what, eight bedrooms?" Brooke asks.

"As it stands now, yes," I reply.

"How many bathrooms?" Brooke asks.

"Too many," I laugh. "Four full bathrooms and two half baths."

"So, it's a huge house. What are your plans for it?" She asks.

"It was my dream growing up to fill it with kids and have a stable on the property with some animals. I wanted to decorate it for Christmas, and maybe, have a haunted house for charity at Halloween. But now…"

I take a deep breath. "Now, I plan to restore it and hope the purpose for the house comes to me. I'll take my last breath in that house. I just know it."

"You're still pretty young, and you can still find a guy and have kids, you know." She says.

I grip Noah's hand and feel him tighten his hold. Though, I'm supposed to be comforting him, I need strength from him.

"Sometimes life throws you a curveball, and you watch your dreams crash and burn around you. Then, you have to find new dreams." I say.

The room is so quiet you can hear a pin drop.

"Sounds like you know from experience," Brooke says softly.

"I do," I whisper.

After a moment, the doctor clears his throat. "Noah, while I have the bandages off do you want a mirror?"

I squeeze his hand, but he doesn't speak.

"Noah?" I ask.

"What do you think I should do, Lexi?"

"Well, this isn't the worst wounds I've seen, and they will get better from here, so it's up to you. You can let them cover the scars back up and see them only after the surgeries, or you can see them now and watch the progress. Either way, I'm not going anywhere."

I feel him take a deep breath. "Okay, let me see," he says.

Brooke moves around, and as much as I want to see him, I keep my head where it is. I want him to know he can trust me.

After a minute, Noah says, "Did they really look worse than this?" I can hear the pain in his voice, and maybe, a little disgust.

"Yes, I've seen burn victims in theater, and the open wounds are much worse." The doctor says.

I take a deep breath "Noah, can I see you? If you say no, I promise I won't look, but... I want to see you."

I feel him go stiff. "There's nothing to see," he says sharply.

50

I go for broke, "I beg to differ. I want to see *you*."

# Chapter 9

**Noah**

I let Lexi's words sink in. She wants to see me.

Can I let her?

She didn't flinch or look disgusted with the burns and scars on my side, but there is something a lot more personal about the scars on my face.

Hell, I'm falling for this girl. I know I am. I don't want her to take one look at me and run. The me who wants to spend more time with her wants to say no.

But the me who wants to protect my heart wants to say yes. Have her leave now, before I fall any further, before I do something stupid, like admit my feelings.

That part wins out.

"Okay," I say.

I feel Lexi smile against my hand. She places a soft kiss on the back of my hand, before lifting her head. I see the doctor and the nurse watching me, and the nurse gives me a smile, trying to ease my nerves.

Before Lexi can turn and look my way, I close my eyes. I don't think I can handle a look of disgust on her face. I want to remember her the way she has looked at me until now like I'm normal.

"Noah, look at me," she says, barely above a whisper.

I don't open my eyes right away still terrified of what I might see, looking back at me in hers.

I know what she sees. The right side of my face was burned and now has twisted scars. My ear is mostly gone, but by the grace of God the fire missed my eye, and I still have my full vision. I haven't processed it all, and I'm not ready to find out how she feels, but I know I can't avoid her forever.

So, I slowly open my eyes and look at the woman who has become everything to me in such a short time. What I see in her face takes my breath away.

I don't see one ounce of disgust or pity. What I see is so close to love that my heart hurts. I can't let myself go there.

"There you are," she says to me in a soft voice. She reaches up and touches my left cheek, the one without all the scars, and I lean into her touch.

"You are beautiful, Noah, and I'll kick anyone's ass who says otherwise." She leans in and kisses my cheek, and the emotion I've been holding back bursts out. I actually cry wrapping my good arm around her and sob.

I cry for the innocent boy going to war who was lost in the desert, I cry for the men wounded that day, I cry for the loss of the one relationship I had clung to, I cry for me, for the scars, I cry for the battle ahead, but mostly, I cry because I can't believe I was sent this astonishing, beautiful woman, even if I can never call her more than my friend.

She rubs my arm but doesn't try to tell me it will be okay. She just lets me get it all out. When I have no more tears, I take a deep breath, and she pulls back and looks at me again.

She smiles and wipes the tears away on my left side, careful not to touch the right side that's still healing. I close my eyes because having her touch my face feels so damn good. But the doctor breaks the moment, clearing his throat.

"We need to clean the wounds and put the bandages back on. In about a week, you should be healed enough to take them off for good. Then, you'll meet with the plastic surgeon and your physical therapist."

I nod. I can't wait to get out of this bed, even if it's for PT. Lexi holds my hand and keeps talking about her house. She knows I need the distraction.

She tells about the wallpaper in the master bedroom, and how she spent a week taking it down, because it gave her the creeps, and she couldn't sleep with it on the walls. She says how she wants to build a garden off to the side and has been trying to find a layout she likes. She wants some herbs and a water fountain and bench.

This girl talking about something so mundane has distracted me perfectly. But she's also intrigued me, and I can only hope I get to see this house one day.

When the doctor and the nurse leave, Lexi scoots the chair close to me, and I bring my hand to her face and hold her cheek.

"Thank you for not running. I was really scared you would," I say, as her face softens.

"Oh, Noah, I'm not going anywhere."

"Why?" I ask. It slips out before I can even think about it, but I need to know.

"Everyone should have someone by their side when they have to fight their way back like this." She says.

"Why you? There are nurses and doctors."

She gives me a sad smile. "At first, it was because I never got the chance, too."

While that answer confuses me, I push her. "And now?"

"Now, I really like you, Noah. You make it easy for me to open up, and it scares me you make it even easier to fall for you." She says the last part in a whisper and lets go of my hand. Then, she rests her elbows on her knees, putting her head in her hands, looking down at the ground.

My heart soars that she feels this connection between us, too. Even the slightest possibility of a chance gives me hope. My heart hammers in my chest, as I think about what she just did.

"What do you mean you never got the chance, too?"

Lexi stands up, and I see tears, pouring down her face. Then, she turns her back to me and goes to look out the window.

Shit. I didn't mean to make her cry, and with her across the room, I can't comfort her. Maybe, that was her intent.

"I was married to a soldier." She starts to speak. "He was everything I wanted and needed. Always took care of me, and I loved that he served, I did. I hated deployments, but we managed well. On his second deployment, his unit was hit by an IED. He died before they could get him to Germany."

I can see her wiping tears off her face, even with her back still to me.

"I buried him at Arlington, as it seemed fitting. He loved it there and always said that it would be an honor to be buried there. I made it happen. I was one of those wives who slept next to her husband's coffin from the moment he was stateside, until the day he was buried. I buried my heart that day, Noah."

She pauses and takes in a shaky breath. "He knew the risks of what he did, and he had a life insurance plan set up for me above and beyond what the military gave me. I bought the house with it. It was my dream, and because he loved me it became his dream, too. He made that happen. I just... I need ..."

She starts crying again.

"Noah, I'll be back, I promise. I just need to not be here right now." She says, gathering her things and walking out of the door.

I have tears in my eyes again. For an entirely new reason. Lexi poured her heart out to me, and it made me realize we had only touched on very safe topics, but so many things make sense now. Some of the comments Moore made, and why she was so pissed off at Whitney. Though, any decent human would have been angry at her, I suspect.

But new questions circle. Was she here for me, or for the experience she never got to have? She did say she could fall for me. That has to mean something, right?

The nurse comes in. "Hey, I saw her leave in tears. I know it's none of my business, but are you okay?"

"Yeah, she just shared a part of her past with me and needs to collect herself. I hate being trapped in this bed. I couldn't even get up to comfort her." I say with more anger in my voice than I mean, too.

"Channel that, when you start PT. You'll need it," she says and walks back out.

I look towards the window, and I feel Lexi's pain. All I can hope is there's room in her heart for me.

# Chapter 10

**Lexi**

Why did I tell Noah all that? This is the last thing I needed today. I can only imagine what he thinks of me now.

I should go home, but instead, I find my way to Johnny's room, tears running down my face, and no way to control them. I go in, and Johnny is sleeping, but Becky takes one look at me and comes over and hugs me tight, just like she knows I need. That's when I really lose it.

No words are spoken. Becky just rubs my back and lets me cry. At some point, I guess my sobbing woke my brother up.

"Lexi?" I hear him ask, his voice still heavy with sleep. "What's wrong? Is Noah okay?"

I take a deep breath and nod, "Noah's fine."

Johnny pats the side of the bed for me to come lie down with him. I climb on and turn to my side facing him, and he turns to face me. We used to do this a lot, when we were kids when one of us wanted to talk. It was sometimes easier to do it in the dark of night, and then we'd fall asleep in whichever bed we were in. Only this time, I don't have the cover of night to hide my feelings.

"What's wrong?" He asks me just above a whisper.

"I told Noah about Tyler," I tell him.

"Oh, shit. How did that come up?" He knows as well as the rest of my family I haven't talked about Tyler, since the day we buried him. I haven't told anyone his story; it's just not talked about.

Thinking about that makes me feel guilty. We should be talking about Tyler daily, but I can't bring myself, too.

"They were changing Noah's bandages, and he wanted me to talk, to distract him, and the first thing that came to mind was the house. I talked about the house and the renovation, and I guess it was just right on the surface. Maybe, part of me needed to put that wall up." I say so quietly that I wasn't sure he heard me, but he did.

"Why?" He asks.

I shake my head, but Johnny waits me out. "Noah let me see him without the bandages on," I say.

"How does he look?" Johnny asks.

"The scars are healing well, and I think he'll be happy after some of the plastic surgery. I just wasn't prepared for how… beautiful he looks, even with all the scars." I pause, gathering my thoughts. "I think it was my way of pushing him away, especially after telling him I could fall for him." I groan and bury my head in Johnny's chest.

"Oh, Lexi," Becky says and rubs my back. "I'm going to go for a walk," she says, and then slips out of the room.

I lay there with Johnny. Neither of us speaking, just listening to the sounds of the TV, as I drift off to sleep.

I wake up later to Becky rubbing my back. "Hey, it's almost dinner time, and you need to eat." She says, holding up some food from the cafeteria for me.

The three of us eat dinner talking about safe topics, mostly making fun of the pawn shop shows Johnny is making us watch.

After dinner, I head back to Noah's room. I've been gone for several hours. I'm nervous about facing him, but I know it needs to be done.

I stand outside his door for a minute to compose myself, and then I take a deep breath and knock on the door.

"Can I come in?" I ask him.

"Lexi, you have never once asked to come in, you just barge in, so why start now?" He says in a playful tone.

"I didn't know if you wanted me here," I say shyly.

He holds his hand out to me. "Of course, I want you here."

I take another deep breath, walk over, and take his hand, sitting down in my chair next to the bed.

I shake my head. "I don't know what to say," I tell him honestly.

"Becky came to see me," he says.

"Well, don't believe everything she says," I grumble, and then I look at him. His blue eyes are brighter today, and he's watching me with a warm look on his face. "What did she say?"

He chuckles, and the sound goes right to my heart. He needs to laugh more, and I want to be here to hear it, when he does. I want to be the cause of his laughs.

"She thanked me."

I look at him confused. "For what?"

"For getting you to open up again. I guess, they've all been really worried about you. She told me a bit of how you were after the funeral." He pauses.

"Oh, you mean, when they wouldn't leave me the hell alone, and then every time I tried to talk, they stuffed horrible tasting food in my mouth? They were the biggest pains in the asses I've ever dealt with." I grumble.

I know in my heart they were worried and wanted to help, and they tried to help in the only ways they knew how, but I just wanted to be left alone. I had to reconfigure my whole life. Figure out what I was going to do. I needed to grieve, and I couldn't do it with my parents, Johnny, Becky, and various people from Tyler's life in and out daily. The only time I had alone time was when I showered. Which I did three or four times a day.

I could see a smile in Noah's eyes.

"And how you didn't get out of bed for a month," he says.

"Well, I had to revise my entire life. I'd like to see her do that, and then get out of bed." I gripe.

"What did you plan?" He asks.

"The house. I found the house, and I knew it's what I was meant to do. I've been focused on that, until I met this guy when I went to go see my brother, who like the idiot he is, got hurt. The guy might have saved said idiot brother and makes me want to spend all my time with him. My house is jealous, and I just know I'm going to come home to something broken any day now."

Every night, I pause at my door and take a deep breath, waiting for something horrible to be wrong. But every day I walk in, and everything is exactly where I left it.

When Tyler was home, I'd get annoyed, when he moved things and wondered why he couldn't leave them alone. Now, everything is always right where I leave it, and I hate it.

Noah laughs now, a really truly carefree belly laugh.

"Tell me about this guy," he says playfully.

My face gets serious. "I need him to know I want to fall for him." I pause and watch his face go somber with something close to love in his eyes. When was the last time someone looked at me like that? Not like I was broken or needed to be fixed, but like I hung the moon.

"I just don't have any pieces of my heart left to give. I buried them in Arlington."

I look away, needing to regroup and get the conversation back on track.

"Tell me about you, please. Distract me, before I lose it again," I say.

He doesn't hesitate and jumps right in to tell me about his parents and his two younger sisters. The conversation leads to how he met Whitney, and how he was comfortable with her. He says he was nerdy in high school and didn't think he'd ever be able to find someone better.

I shake my head at that. "Noah, never settle. Settling kills your soul."

He nods, and we fall into an easy conversation until visiting hours are up.

Heading home that night, I feel lighter than I have for a long time, and I catch myself smiling more and more.

# Chapter 11

## Lexi

Over the next week, we fall into a comfortable routine. I spend the day with him working. We talk about what I'm doing, or what is on TV. He says he just wants something to concentrate on, and he likes the sound of my voice.

When I cuss at emails I have to deal with, he laughs and likes giving his opinion, when I edit photos. I find myself more productive working with Noah than I am at home.

We have both become friends with his nurse, Brooke, and she has been spending time in his room, during her breaks just hanging out with us.

I told Noah last night I'd be in later today, as I needed to shoot some photos, and I don't get in, until lunchtime. I consider bringing some food in for Noah, but they have been easing him on to solid foods, so I don't think it would be a good idea just yet.

When I walk into his room and see Noah, I stop in my tracks. He's sitting up in bed wearing sweatpants and a t-shirt with his legs stretched out and crossed at the ankle. This is the first time I've seen him in something other than a hospital gown since all this started. Noah in everyday clothes is hot as hell!

But that's not what shocks me the most. Today, his bandages are off. I look at him and see his scars are white and pink against his skin from his temple down past his neck. His hair has grown out, and even though I saw him without his bandages just over a week ago, I wasn't prepared for this.

Noah is watching me look him over, waiting for me to say something. I can see the uncertainty in his eyes, and I know he's uncomfortable, waiting for my reaction.

"You have to ease a girl into this," I say. "Your bandages off, and you in regular clothes all at once were enough to make my heart stop. You look damn sexy, Noah."

He blushes and then looks down at his hands in his lap. He blushed, because of me! That's a powerful feeling. One I haven't felt in a while. In that moment, a small piece of my heart is healed, something I thought was gone forever. Noah's vulnerability was such a damn turn on.

I put my stuff down and walk over to him never taking my eyes off him. He still hasn't said anything, so I sit down on the side of his bed. He looks up at me because this isn't something I've done before. I haven't sat on the side of his bed. I was too afraid to hurt him, while he had the bandages on.

He still hasn't made eye contact with me, and I can't have that.

"Noah, look at me," I say softly. When his eyes meet mine, I ask, "What's wrong?"

"You'll keep visiting me, right?"

"Oh, Noah, of course, I will. And when you get out of here, you will have to come visit me and keep me company, while I battle that big old house."

He gives me a half smile, "I'd like that."

"Is that what you were worried about?" I ask, looking him over. I can tell he's holding something back.

I sigh, "Noah, I want to make you a deal." I pause and wait for him.

When he looks up at me, I continue, "You're the first person I've told about Tyler, so I'll make a pact with you. No secrets. If you will be my person I can share with, the good and the bad, and no matter how stupid it is, then let me be that person for you."

He pauses and looks at me and says, "No secrets?"

"No secrets," I reply.

"I'm scared to be alone here."

I grab his hand. "You won't be. I promise to make sure, if at any point I can't be here, I'll make sure someone is. I wouldn't want to be alone here either."

He smiles at me, looking a lot more relaxed.

"Now, tell me what the doctor said."

"I meet with the plastic surgeon next week. The doctor wanted me to be prepared for the time it will take. It'll be a long road because each surgery has to heal before they can do the next. Later today, I meet with the physical therapist, but I won't start until I get the okay from the plastic surgeon. I asked him to try to remove me from as much medication as possible, so he put me on pain medicine as needed. If I want the meds from now on, I'll have to ask for them. He's making me take a bunch of vitamins, and I'm going to try to go without the sleeping medicine. I don't want to be dependent on this stuff, and he agreed."

I smile at him, "I'm so proud of you. Not everyone is strong enough to do that, especially so early on."

We settle into a comfortable conversation until the physical therapist comes in.

She does some basic assessments on his leg and arm strength, and then says, "The first goal is getting in and out of bed by yourself. Then, being able to maneuver around the room."

"Anything I can do to help?" I ask.

She smiles at me, "Actually there is. Come here."

She shows me how to hold my palms flat up and let Noah push against them, and then do the same with his legs. We have a few rounds of practice.

"I know it seems small, but it's a good way for him to build his strength back and both of you'll notice it. Do that a few times a day."

I nod. When she heads out, Noah looks happy.

"You okay?" I ask.

"Yeah, it's nice to be moving forward. Before, it was a lot of waiting. Now, I can actually start doing something."

I laugh. "Hurry up and wait. The military motto."

He smiles.

I leave just after dinner and go over to see Johnny. I fill him in on Noah and then ask how he's doing. He's been learning to walk in a prosthetic.

"So, why exactly aren't you home and learning how to do this?" I ask him.

He shares a look between him and Becky.

"Just tell me," I say, thinking it's something bad.

"It's not bad," Johnny says, reading my mind.

"It's just I'm still unsteady and need help with some things, and well…" he trails off.

"I'm pregnant," Becky says.

I'm going to be an aunt. Visions of baby clothes shopping fill my head, and then it hits me. This could have been me.

We were going to try for a baby when Tyler got back from deployment. I take a deep breath and remind myself I've been preparing for this day.

"How far along are you?" I ask.

"Only a few weeks," she says.

Then it clicks. She wasn't pregnant in Germany.

"Yuck! I'm so telling this baby it was conceived in the hospital." I say grossed out.

They laugh at me, and I head towards the door.

"Ugh! I'm out of here," I say.

"Don't tell Mom and Dad. We're going to surprise them." Johnny says.

"Let me know when. I want to see their faces when they connect the dots!" I say and walk out.

Before I know it, I'm back at Noah's room.

"Hey, I thought you went home," Noah says.

"I went to see Johnny, and now, I need brain bleach," I say, as I go sit in the chair next to his bed. I cross my hands over my chest, like a toddler, who just had her favorite toy taken away.

"You okay?" He asks concerned.

"Oh, yeah. Johnny is up and working with his prosthetic, but then, I ask why he isn't home yet, and they tell me it's cause Becky is pregnant."

"That's good news, right?"

"She's only a few weeks pregnant..." I trail off.

He starts laughing. Full on belly laughing.

"It's not funny. I love them, but *knowing* the baby was conceived in the hospital, and in that bed, I'm creeped out. I don't need to *know* where it happened. Just that it happened." I say and shiver.

Noah is laughing, and I can't help but laugh, too. It's the first time I've seen him laugh like this, so carefree. I look at him truly happy, and my heart clenches. He's so handsome, scars and all, and I know right here, right now, I'm falling for him.

# Chapter 12

## Lexi

*I'm falling for Noah.*

That thought has been racing around in my head ever since I walked out of his room tonight. The entire drive home, that's all I can think about.

This one thought scared the hell out of me. By the time I pull into my driveway, I know I need to go see Tyler.

As I head inside, I call Becky, because no matter what I'm feeling, I won't break my promise to Noah.

"Hey, I need you and Johnny to go hang out with Noah tomorrow," I tell Becky. I'm walking to my room and packing a bag at the same time, and I know she can tell something is up.

"Why what's wrong?"

"I'm going out of town."

"Everything okay?" She asks concerned.

"Yes. No. I don't know."

"Hey, breathe," she says, and I take a deep breath.

"I'm going to Arlington." Becky doesn't need to ask why, because she knows.

"Need company? I can have Johnny hang out with Noah tomorrow, and we can go together."

Before I even have time to think about it, I say, "Yes."

"Okay, I'll be there in thirty minutes," she says, hanging up.

True to her word, thirty minutes later she's pulling into my driveway. I go outside, and we place both our bags in the back seat of my car. She hugs me, and we head out.

It's an eight hour drive, but being able to even drive a few hours tonight, will save us time tomorrow. We talk about her pregnancy and make fun of some of the roadside signs. After driving for three hours, we pull over at the North Carolina-South Carolina border, where the South of the Border amusement area is and grab a hotel for the night.

Though, we're up early and ready the next morning, Becky gets hit by morning sickness. While she throws up, I'm holding her hair, like any best friend would do.

"In my purse, there's a lollipop. Get it for me, please?"

"Little early for candy but okay," I say and find the lollipop she asked for.

After a minute of sucking on it, she smiles.

"These are special lollipops for morning sickness, and they work like a charm. Let me clean up, and I'll be good to go." She says.

I shrug my shoulders, and we hit the road. We drive another six hours with stops for Becky to pee and to grab food and gas.

We pull into the hotel I always stay at, while I'm here and check in. We drop our bags in our room, and then head right back out and make our way to the cemetery.

Like always, I first pay my respects to the Tomb of the Unknown Soldier and watch the changing of the guards. Then, my feet carry me past the rows and rows of matching headstones. It would be so easy to get lost here, but my feet know the way.

They know which path to take. Around the tree and up the hill. Another right turn, three rows up, fourth headstone in. Right there engraved on the headstone that looks just like every other headstone here, is the name I see every night before I go to sleep.

Tyler Bates
    Staff Sargent, U.S. Marine Corps
    Afghanistan. Iraq.
    July 16, 1993
    April 23, 2017
    Husband. Son. Brother.

I don't know how long I stand there, but I stand there so long I can't see the headstone anymore. I'm seeing the day I hugged him goodbye for the last time. The last time I ever saw him alive.

We had plans to start a family when he got home from deployment. We were so excited talking about baby names before he left. Part of me wishes we had started trying sooner, so I'd have a piece of him here with me now.

The bigger part of me is happy a child won't have to suffer from him being gone, growing up without a dad. Happy a child never had to watch me go through the pain of losing my soul mate. Happy a child will never look at this headstone and say that's my dad and wonder what he was like.

In the distance, the start of a 21 Gun Salute goes off, and I lose it. Falling to my knees, I start crying. I cried for the future plans we made that would never come true, and the future I lost. I cry for all the memories that flood me of the day when those twenty-one guns went off for this man. Becky is right there holding me. Rubbing my back, but never speaking. I vaguely hear an older man ask her if I'm okay.

I cry through the whole thing and then lay down on the grass like I was lying down next to Tyler. Becky sits behind me, there for comfort but quietly, letting me mourn. She rests her hand on top of my head and plays with my hair.

We must sit there for over an hour before I finally start talking to Tyler. I tell him about the house and all the improvements I've done since I was here seven months ago. I tell him about Johnny and Noah. I tell him everything down to finding out about Becky being pregnant and telling Noah.

When I tell him about watching Noah laugh, I have a huge smile on my face. Suddenly, Becky I are laughing, too. Then, my smile fades, and I say what I came here to say.

"I'm falling for him, and I don't know what, too."

As I'm wiping my eyes, a woman a little older than me has sat down on the other side of Tyler's grave, and a man stands just behind her.

"I'm sorry I couldn't help but overhear you, and you can tell me to fuck off, but I feel maybe I was supposed to be here in this moment. Though, I hadn't planned to visit today, I felt I needed to be here. I'm Kim."

She pauses and points a few rows over. "That's my Greg. We were married at eighteen. We grew up together, and I met him when I was five. He was my best friend, and later, my soul mate. We lived in a small-town with not a lot of opportunities, so he decided to enlist."

I sit up and listen to her story. Early on, I learned we all share the same scars here at Arlington, and it's therapy to tell your story and to hear other's stories. Every story I've heard, I have gained insight. The bonds here are like nowhere else on earth.

"Being away from him during boot camp and training was the worst. It was our first real time apart. But when he got his orders, we moved into military housing. We were one of the lucky few and had two years together, before his first deployment. He was gone eight months that time, and when he came home, it was like he had never left."

She pauses and stares off, no doubt lost in the memory.

"Six months later, he went back again, and this time for only four months to fill in, where they were shorthanded. We had been saving money and planned on buying a house with the money from our next assignment. He came home from that deployment with a few scars, but nothing big. We went another two years without a deployment. Then, the last time, he didn't make it home. They called it friendly gunfire, but you and I both know there was nothing friendly about it." She gives me a watery smile.

"It killed me. I didn't get out of bed for a month. Well, you know the drill. I'm sure we all find our ways to move forward and make those around us think we are okay when we aren't."

I feel Becky's hand squeeze my shoulder. What she said was true, you simply get better at hiding it, and Becky knows she's right.

"About four years after his death, I was just getting by on my own. I was in my own world, in my own routine, and in barges this guy." She points over her shoulder, as he kneels down and places a hand on her shoulder.

"A few months after meeting him, I was right where you are, begging him to forgive me for falling for another man. I felt like I was being unfaithful. It was another wife who was here that day that told me I wasn't. She asked me if it was me in the ground, and he found someone to make him smile again if I thought he was being unfaithful. I didn't answer her, I couldn't. But she knew." Kim smiles.

"She then told me it was Greg, leading Brett to me. She believed our husbands who passed had picked who they want to take care of us." At this point, both Kim and I have tears, streaming down our faces.

"When you think you've buried your heart, think of this. A mother doesn't love her kids any less than the new baby who is just born. Her heart grows. Your heart is growing right now. Your young man is giving you a piece of his to heal you, and I fully believe he was handpicked by your Tyler."

She pauses again and squeezes Brett's hand. "We have been together for five years and married for four now. He doesn't push Greg away, he embraces him. Not only do we have photos in the house, but he brings me here at the drop of a hat."

Brett smiles, and then says, "The right guy will understand and accept Tyler. He won't ever ask you to give him up, but he'll be by your side and understand the life you had planned and respect it. I know Kim loves me, but I know she loves him too and always will. I'm okay with that."

He smiles at Kim, "The way I see it, he kept her safe and loved for the first part of her life. I'm meant to love her the second part of it."

I can't help but smile at that. We sit and talk for a bit and exchange phone numbers to stay in touch. They walk back out to the parking lot, and Becky goes with them since she has to pee, yet again. I tell her I'll meet her at the car.

As she walks away, I say to her, "Call Johnny and ask him to go see Noah again tomorrow, please."

She smiles and nods.

I sit there with Tyler a bit longer, trying to think how I would feel if the situation was reversed. Then, a distant memory comes back to me. One I had forgotten until now. Many nights, before deployment, we'd lay in bed talking about everything and anything. Since every deployment was different, we both never knew what to expect. But this one night, I remember the conversation clearly.

*"Lexi, I need you to promise me something," Tyler said, his voice serious.*

*"Anything, you know that," I said, lifting my head from his shoulder to look at him.*

*"If something happens to me, I want you to be happy. I want you to love again and find someone who loves you as hard as I do."*

*"Stop talking like that," I said, laying my head back down, not able to look at him.*

*A split second later, he rolls me over on top of me and has me pinned down on the bed. His eyes bore into mine.*

*"I'm serious, Lexi. I don't want you to go through the rest of your life alone. I want you to allow someone to love you again. I want you to open your heart and allow yourself to love them."*

*Then, I had burst out into tears. "I can't," I sobbed.*

*He gave me a sad smile. "You will. I'll make sure of it. I want you to have all your dreams, Lexi. Every damn one of them, and I will make that happen. Promise me, Lexi. Promise me, you will move on and be happy. You will buy your house and fill it with kids and grandkids and keep doing your photography and be happy. Promise me." He says, pleading.*

*"I promise." I finally said, sobbing again.*

I cry now, because I know it was him bringing Kim to me today, and it was him bringing that memory back. I lean up to the headstone and rest my forehead against the smooth, cold stone.

"I love you with my whole heart and made you a promise I never thought I'd have to keep. But I will try my best. I love you and thank you for bringing Noah to me. I'll see you in the morning."

I take a deep breath and kiss the stone, before making my way back to my car.

# Chapter 13

**Lexi**

When I get back to my car, Becky wraps up her phone call.

"You okay if we come back and visit tomorrow before we head out?" I ask her.

"Of course." She smiles.

I try to force a smile, but of course, she can see right through that.

"You okay?" She asks.

"Yeah, I remembered a conversation we had, before his first deployment. You know where you sit and talk about anything and everything because you don't know what to expect? I just… feel at peace now." I say.

"Good." She smiles at me.

Once at the hotel, we decide to grab take out from the pizza place across the street and eat in the room.

"Why don't you go take a shower? I'll go get the food. Still like sausage, onions, and green pepper now that you're pregnant?" I ask.

"Yes, and breadsticks. Oh, and a soda!" She says as I head out the door.

When I get back with the food, I find Becky, relaxing on her bed. Her dark brown hair wet and curly.

I sit on the bed, and we spread out the food.

"Oh, man. This pizza is really good," Becky says.

"Yeah, it's the highlight of visiting up here," I say, bringing the conversation to a crashing halt.

We eat in silence for a few minutes, before Becky starts talking again.

"Johnny spent the day with Noah. He says Noah kept asking where you were, and if you were okay. Johnny didn't know what to tell him, said you had something to do, that you were fine, and I was with you. I guess, they watched TV and played some cards, but Noah was distracted the whole time, almost sad."

I don't know what to say, so I keep eating.

"Noah asked about you, how you were as a kid and Johnny's favorite memories of you. And I shouldn't tell you this, but I think you should know in light of today. Noah asked Johnny's permission to date you if the opportunity arises." She says.

I almost choke on my pizza.

"What did Johnny say?" I ask.

"He gave his permission."

A huge smile takes over my face.

"They also talked a bit about their next steps. You know they're both being honorably discharged. They'll be one hundred percent disabled, so they have those payments to lean on. Johnny's talking about flipping houses with your dad. Noah wants to go back to school, but he hasn't decided what for yet."

I like the idea of Noah doing something he wants.

"One more thing."

"Good lord, was I really gone that long?" I ask, and she laughs.

"There's talk about both guys getting some service medals. They'll wait, until they are out of the hospital to awarded, of course. Johnny wasn't the only one Noah saved. That's all Johnny would say. I guess, they haven't told Noah yet, because Johnny is worried he's not ready to hear it or to talk about that day."

I nod lost in thought. This won't be my first ceremony. Tyler received a purple heart that I accepted in his place after he died. It's in the shadow box above the fireplace in my living room and has his flag displayed in it.

We talk some more just like old times. She tells me about the pregnancy book she's reading, and we laugh really hard at some of the pregnancy side effects. It feels good to laugh again.

After we finish dinner, Becky steps outside to go sit in the car and call Johnny. I try to watch TV but can't concentrate.

So, I pick up my phone and call the hospital. I get put through to Noah's room. It rings for a while before he picks up.

"Hello?" He answers hesitantly.

"Noah, it's Lexi."

"Lexi," he sighs.

"Do you want... can you talk?" I ask unsure if he wants to talk to me.

"Yeah, I've got nothing but time." He says, and then we're both quiet.

"Where are you? Is everything okay?"

"I'm fine, I promise. I'm actually better than I have been in a long time, and I'll promise to tell you everything next time I see you."

78

He hesitates for a moment, "When will that be?"

"Day after tomorrow. Johnny is going to hang out with you again tomorrow. Is that okay? If not, I can find someone else, but be warned it will probably be my mother, and trust me, you want to pick Johnny."

He chuckles.

"Johnny and I already have plans."

"Good. So, tell me about your day."

"Johnny made me watch God awful TV shows about pawn shops." He says.

I laugh, "He has like five different ones he watches. I always zone out, when they are on."

"So, did I. We played some cards and talked, too."

"Did you do your PT exercises?"

"Yeah, Brooke helped me."

Shoot, I should have called and told her I wasn't going to be there, so she'd keep an eye on him.

"Good," I say.

It's quiet for a moment, but not uncomfortable.

When he speaks again, it's barely above a whisper. "Are you sure you're okay?"

"I wasn't when I left last night, but... people are put in your path when you need them the most. Today, proved that, yet again. And right now, I'm doing really well. Becky and I had dinner, and we laughed. I don't remember laughing that much in a long time."

When he speaks again, I can hear the smile in his voice. "Good, I like it, when you laugh."

"Noah..." I sigh not sure of my words.

"Yeah, angel?" He says.

The term of endearment is exactly what gives me the

strength to say what's on my mind.

"I miss you," I say.

He takes a deep shaky breath. "I miss you, too. So much."

Things are quiet for a moment, but it's an easy quiet.

"Lexi?"

"Yeah?"

"I need a favor."

"Anything, Noah."

"Well, they're discharging me from the Marines, and I was staying on base in the barracks. They're boxing up my stuff, and I need help getting it out of there." He says.

"Done. I'll enlist a few friends to help. We'll move it to my place because I have plenty of storage."

"You sure?"

"Promise. Just let me know when and where, and I'll be there." I tell him.

"Becky will need to get you on the base." He adds.

"Did you forget I'm a widow? I get base privileges for life to use the doctor or commissary, all that fun stuff. How do you think I was able to come to see you every day?"

"I thought you were getting visitor passes."

"Nope." I laugh. "Just let me know the date and time, and I'll make it happen, okay?"

"Thank you."

"You're welcome."

I hear Becky inserting her key in the door, so I decide to wrap up my call.

"Hey, Becky is back, and we'll have an early morning tomorrow. So, I'll talk to you tomorrow night. Okay?" I say.

"Fine, be safe, Lexi."

"I will. Bye, Noah."

After we hang up, I look up to find Becky, watching me with a big grin.

"I was hoping you'd call him. He was really missing you." She says.

"Well, we need to rally the troops. Noah has to get his stuff out of the barracks, and I told him he can store it at my place." I tell her.

Becky nods. "I'll get the details and have Johnny reach out to a few guys."

"Thanks. How's the collection for Noah's family coming along?"

"We have the money for the plane tickets for all four of them."

"And they can stay with me, so that takes care of lodging."

"We're still raising money to cover their loss of income for taking some time off. From what Johnny tells me, they are barely making it paycheck to paycheck, and any missed time would sink them." She says.

I just nod.

"I have a few more tricks up my sleeve. You leave it to me." Becky jumped into military life with both feet. She made connections and learned everything she could. She volunteered and helped out a lot. Even more so, once Tyler died. After that, I stepped away and lost most of my connections. Thankfully, Becky is here to help.

I had planned to be alone today, but I'm really glad she's here.

# Chapter 14

**Lexi**

I'm up, before the sun the next day, just like I always am, when I'm here, standing at the window just watching the city come to life. Becky gets up to use the restroom, and then stands by me, as watch the sunrise. It's barely five a.m.

You might expect my mind to be racing, but it's actually blank. I'm calm and at peace right now. A feeling I have, when I'm here.

"You know, if we get going now, we can get back in time to see the guys, before visiting hours are up tonight." She says.

I like the idea of surprising Noah. Everything has changed for us in the last few days and in the best way.

I smile. "You ready to head out?"

"Yep, just got to get dressed."

Once we are dressed and everything is loaded into the car, I check us out of the hotel, and we grab a quick breakfast from a food cart a few blocks down from the hotel. Breakfast tacos are seriously the best, and bonus, little baby no name likes them, so no morning sickness for Becky.

We head to Arlington Cemetery and park. We have enough

time to eat and make it for the Changing of the Guard. After watching the ceremony, we head to see Tyler again.

Today, is a good day. I feel so much better. It's a night and day difference from when I made this same walk yesterday.

I come to a stop in front of his headstone. "I remember the promise I made you. It's not easy, Tyler. It fucking sucks, but I'm going to try. For you, I'm going to try. I talked to Noah last night, and it was lighter. He's easy to talk to just like you were, and it's hard to hold my secrets with him."

Pausing, I remember how Tyler could always pull any information out of me. There were never any secrets between us, and we could talk to each other about anything. He was my best friend, my partner.

"I know you brought Noah to me. The same way you brought Kim to me yesterday. Thank you. I know you're watching out for me, and I'll try to make you proud."

Before I start crying again, I take a moment to get myself together. Becky places her hand on my back, lending me her strength.

"I promise to come back for your birthday like I always do. If Noah is able to make the trip, I'll bring him, too."

After I kiss the headstone, Becky and I walk hand-in-hand to the car. We start the long drive home, but by the grace of God, we don't hit any traffic. It's like Tyler is saying you must see Noah. He knows I need to just as much as I have the feeling that I do.

We grab some fast food for dinner, eat, and then go back to my place, so Becky can get her car. Then, we head over to surprise the guys.

"Johnny said he's back in his room, so we'll see you in a bit," Becky tells me at Noah's door.

I stand just outside his door and take a deep breath. This is the same hospital, the same room, and the same guy, but everything feels different. Everything is different because I'm different now. In the best way.

When I peek my head in, Noah's sitting on his bed, looking out the window. He looks sad and tired. I knock on the door frame, and his head snaps to me, and his whole face lights up.

Right here, this moment right now is life changing in so many more ways than I can describe. Someone was waiting for me, and I made him smile. Those are powerful feelings when you had resigned yourself to being alone for the rest of your life.

"We got in early, so I thought I'd surprise you," I say, as he scoots over and pats the side of the bed.

I hesitantly walk over to the bed but don't sit.

"Best surprise ever." He smiles, and I can't take my eyes off of him. Where he looked sad moments ago, he looks happier and lighter than the last time I saw him, which was less than forty-eight hours ago.

"Sit with me?" He asks, patting the bed again.

I slowly sit down beside him, making sure I don't hurt him. This is the closest we have ever been. He takes my hand and holds it on his lap. I look over at him and give him a small smile. He smiles back, as our eyes lock.

We're so close I'm touching him from my shoulder to my hip, and every single inch tingles. My skin that's touching his skin feels like it's on fire. He moves towards me slowly, until his forehead rests on mine. He doesn't take it any further. We just sit there, soaking each other in.

"I missed you," I whisper to him, needing him to know I was thinking of him on my trip.

"I missed you too, angel, so much." He whispers back.

He brings his scarred hand to my cheek and slowly pushes it into my hair, before closing the distance between us. A moment later his lips are on mine, and the world tilts and time slows. This kiss stops the world from spinning, exactly how Becky told me she felt, when she kissed Johnny for the first time, how it felt, when I first kissed Tyler, and how my mom says it felt when she first kissed my dad.

Noah's lips on mine feel incredible. As I kiss him back, I explore the soft mixed with the rough scars on one side. The mix of the rough and soft turn me on so damn much that I didn't think it was possible. Neither of us are in hurry to speed this kiss up. We both want to enjoy the moment.

Without thinking, I reach up and place my hand on his cheek, and his entire body stiffens. That's when I realize my hand is on his scarred cheek.

# Chapter 15

**Noah**

I'm so lost in the sexiest kiss of my life that I don't realize what Lexi is doing until her hand touches my face. I don't think she realized what she was doing either by the way she stiffened up.

Not sure what her response will be, I pull back slightly and go still. She shocks me when she leans in to kiss me again, and this time bringing her other hand up to place on the other side of my cheek. Then, I rest my forehead on hers.

Her hand on my scarred side feels so good, so right. I'm too scared to let her keep going, but also too scared to pull away because that was the best damn kiss of my life. I never knew a kiss could be this intense. The way she kissed me back. Holy hell, I just don't have the words.

Keeping her forehead to mine, her fingers start tracing the scars, and I'm frozen, unable to move, even if I wanted, too. Her touching the scars makes me uncomfortable, but she's the only person I trust enough to let touch them. *Only her.* So, I fight the instinct to pull back and let her gently stroke my scars.

Clamping my eyes closed, I concentrate on my breathing, but when she kisses my forehead, I forget how to breathe. Her soft lips move down the scared side of my face, kissing the grooves and raised skin, and fuck, if she doesn't break me right then.

Any worry I have of how she looks at me is gone. She just showed me how she feels. She kisses down my cheek slowly, not leaving an inch of skin untouched. When she reaches my jawline, she kisses her way back to my mouth.

Then, her lips land back on mine, and my hand is pulling her into me to kiss her, as deeply as I can. In this kiss, I pour out my emotions I'm afraid to say, and the ones I can't find the words to say. I claim her in this kiss, even if she isn't ready to hear it, but she has become mine.

When we pull away, we are both breathless, and I look into her eyes. She's a little dazed, but she offers me a soft smile. I love that I can make her look like that.

"Will you lay with me and tell me about your trip?" I ask.

"Okay." She smiles at me.

I adjust the bed and lay off to one side. She lies down and rests her head on my shoulder. I wrap my arm around her and hold her to me, and she presses her chest to my side, and her legs rest against my leg.

Having her in my arms for the first time, makes everything go away. The pain, the suffering from the accident, the anxiety of not having a way to take care of my parents, the last few days of her being gone, and the surgeries coming up. All of it melts always with her in my arms.

"Tell me, angel." I encourage her to talk, but I don't want to push her. When we talked last night on the phone, I hadn't meant to call her angel. In my head, I've been thinking of her as my angel, but I hadn't meant to say it out loud. Now that I have, I don't think I can stop.

I firmly believe that when Whitney walked out, if Lexi hadn't been there and given me something to fight for, I wouldn't be here today. *Lexi is my angel.*

"So, the other day, when we were in here laughing about Becky and Johnny being pregnant and all?" She says.

I smile at the memory of her laughing. "Yeah?"

"I don't remember being that happy in a really long time, and I realized…" She pauses, unsure of continuing.

I want to hear it all. I want her to trust me.

"No secrets," I say to her.

She sighs, "No secrets." She agrees.

"I realized watching you laugh like that how much… how much I was falling for you. Then, I was immediately racked with guilt."

I stiffen not sure which way this is going to go. She was feeling guilty, and then, I kissed her. What's she feeling now?

She rubs my chest, "I promise, I'm good now. Just listen, okay?"

"All right," I say, tucking her head under my chin and holding her a bit tighter, as much to offer her support, as to reassure myself she's still here.

"So, I made a split second decision to go up to Arlington National Cemetery and see Tyler. I didn't know then what I needed, but I just knew I needed to be there. Then, I called Becky and asked her and Johnny to come to sit with you, but she knows me too well. She asked if I wanted company, and I knew I didn't want to be alone, so I said yes, and she was at my house thirty minutes later."

She pauses, almost lost in thought, before continuing. "We

drove until we had to stop that night, and then finished the drive the next day. Got a hotel room, dropped off our bags, and then we went straight to Arlington Cemetery, to the Changing of the Guard. I always go to that first."

I rub her back, letting her know I'm here for her, but also because I don't want to stop touching her.

"I don't remember walking to his grave, but there I was and instantly remembered the last time I saw him. Unfortunately, I didn't know there was a funeral there that day, and when the 21-Gun Salute went off, I lost it. It's my trigger." She whispers the last part.

I hold her tight and close my eyes. The last thing she needs to see are the tears in my eyes because I can only imagine what she has been through. What I was so close to putting my family through if it wasn't for Lexi.

"After crying for I don't know how long, Becky just sat there with me. Finally, I laid down next to him, and I told him about you. I shared everything."

I'm sure she can hear my heart racing in my chest, and she confirms it when she turns her head and places a kiss right there. Suddenly, I wish the shirt wasn't in the way.

"I told him everything. Every little detail, down to seeing you laugh and falling for you. Then, I cried some more, because I felt so guilty. He was listening to every word; I know it because a woman sat down on the other side of me. She said she had been in my shoes. Her now husband stood there with her, as she told me she hadn't planned to come that day, but had this overwhelming need, too. When she told me her story, I could relate, because it was so close to mine. Then, she asked if the situation was reversed would I feel like he was cheating on me. I couldn't answer her, as I had never thought of it that way."

When she starts lightly tracing the design on my shirt, the sensation is too much. I reach over with my scarred hand and hold her hand. She doesn't flinch or pull away, but tightly holds my hand, like she's afraid I'll pull away.

"The woman said she was told by another girl at the cemetery that when you start to fall in love again, it's your spouse sending you to the one he wants to take care of you. After that, we exchanged phone numbers to keep in touch, and Becky left to go call Johnny. I sat there thinking. What if it was me in the ground? I know I'd want him to be happy, to live life, find love again, and be loved. Then, out of nowhere, a memory came to me of a night before Tyler's first deployment. One I had forgotten about."

She snuggles up to me getting even closer, before continuing, "We were lying in bed, much like this, and just talking about anything and everything. Neither of us knew what to expect other than what Johnny and Becky had been through. They had one deployment under their belt, and this was our first. That night he said if anything happened to him, he wanted me to be happy. I told him to stop talking like that, and I can see his face as clearly as if he were sitting here today. His face was stone cold serious. He was insistent that I find someone to love again. To allow it, so I didn't go through the rest of my life alone. He said he wanted to make my dreams come true, the house, kids, grandkids, photography, all of it. Then, he made me promise, and I did because I never thought I'd have to keep it. Again, on the last night before he left, he made me vow that I'd keep my promise."

My mind is racing. What does this mean? I have so many questions I want to ask, but I'm too scared and worried she'll run.

"So, that night, Becky and I got some pizza in the hotel room, and we sat and talked. We laughed, and it was just like old times before she was with my brother. Before the military, and it was just two best friends, giggling about boys and school. I can't remember the last time I laughed so much. Then, I called you, and the guilt was gone. We went and saw Tyler again this morning before we left. I thanked him for bringing you into my life. You think you needed me that day, but I needed you just as bad. Then, I promised him I'd bring you next time, which is in five months for his birthday."

I smile, five months is a good goal, because I'd love nothing more than to go with her.

"I don't want to replace him."

"I know you don't. That's part of the guilt I had that it was me replacing him by loving someone again, but it isn't replacing him. It's carrying on his memory." We are both quiet for a bit before she speaks again.

"He will always be a part of my life and out in the open. I won't hide him away and pack up his photos. You okay with that?" She asks.

I kiss the top of her head, "I wouldn't have it any other way."

# Chapter 16

**Noah**

"Now, your turn, why do you look so tired? Are you not sleeping?" She asks.

I really didn't want to get into this, but it's like she can tell I'm trying to find a way to avoid the topic.

"No secrets, Noah."

"No secrets." I agree.

"I stopped with the sleeping medication, but now, I'm not in that deep medicated sleep, and it has brought back nightmares from the explosion," I tell her.

"Do you want to talk about it?"

I know I will have to talk to my therapist about it before I'm discharged, but I know if we are going to have a fighting chance, I'll have to talk to Lexi, too.

"Not right now, but soon," I say because I'm not ready to open that can of worms just yet.

"Okay. Noah?" She says.

"Hmm?"

"I don't think I ever thanked you."

"For what, angel?"

"For saving my brother."

It feels like I was just punched in the gut, and if I had been standing up, I know I'd have crumpled to the ground. My eyes water and I clamp them shut to prevent myself from crying. I look up at the ceiling and get my emotions under control before I speak.

"I did what anyone would have done," I tell her.

"But it wasn't anyone, it was you."

My throat burns, as I continue to fight off the tears.

"I'd do it all over again, because it brought you to me, and I can never be sorry for that." Needing to change the subject, I tell her what else I was doing.

"So, I met another patient, while you were gone," I tell her.

"Yeah?"

"Brooke came in and said it would do me some good to get out of my room, so she got me a wheelchair, and we went for a walk in the halls. While she was talking to another nurse, I saw him sitting in his room, facing the window. His name is Easton, and he won't let anyone in his room." I tell her.

"Why not?"

"He didn't say, but I found out that he was kept as a prisoner of war for a year. Though, all his physical wounds are healed, mentally, he's still not okay. So, they won't release him. But he did let me sit at the doorway and talk to him. Although, he didn't talk much, I told him about you and about your brother. He said a few words, and I promised I'd come back to see him again."

"I'd like to meet him." She says right before she yawns.

I hold her a bit tighter, thankful that she's my reason to fight. A few minutes later she's asleep. She has had a long few days, so I refuse to wake her up. I love that she feels safe enough

93

with me to fall asleep, and I adore having her in my arms like this, too.

She deserves so much more than this hospital room. I wish I could take her out on a real date, and wine and dine her like she deserves. I should be taking care of her, but instead, she's here every day taking care of me. But I heard her when she said she needed me, too.

After we got off the phone last night, I fell hard for this beautiful angel in my arms. I'm already in love with her. I'd do anything for her, including bust my ass to get better, so I can take her on a proper date and to take care of her if she will let me. Though, I still have to talk to her about what the doctor said about me and sex and having kids, but for now, I'll be content to sit here and watch over her, while she sleeps. How can I not enjoy her body pressed against mine?

There's a soft knock on the door before the nighttime nurse pokes her head in. She sees Lexi and smiles.

"I don't see anything. Just let me get your vitals, and then you should get some sleep. I'm willing to bet she's the one keeping your nightmares away." The nurse says.

"What do you mean?"

"I see it all the time. The one you trust most is the one you feel safest with, and that's who is the one who keeps the nightmares away." She writes a few things down on her tablet, and then pats my arm and walks out.

I hope she's right. I rest my head on top of Lexi's and close my eyes.

The next thing I know, Lexi is shifting around.

"Angel, sit still," I mumble without even opening my eyes.

"Noah, what time is it?" She asks a bit groggy.

I look over at the clock on my nightstand.

"8:24 a.m." I tell her.

She sits straight up in bed. "Why didn't the nurse wake me?" She says, combing her fingers through her hair.

I chuckle, "She came in and took my vitals and told me to go to sleep and enjoy it. Angel, come back here." I hold my hand back out to her.

She takes it and lies back down with me.

"I need you to know how amazing you are," I tell her, kissing the top of her head.

"Noah…" She starts, but I keep talking.

"I slept through the night. No nightmares with you in my arms."

"Good. Now, I'm going to go home and shower and change, unpack and eat breakfast. I'll be back in two hours tops."

"Wear something comfy. I want to snuggle some more," I tell her.

She smiles and nods, as I watch her walk out of the door. Brooke comes in right behind her.

"How did you sleep?" She asks.

"Like a baby."

Brooke laughs, "We all thought you would. Just don't tell anyone we let her stay, okay?"

"Not a word."

"How long have you two been together?" She asks as she starts looking over my vitals.

"I don't think we're actually together," I say and cringe at how it sounds.

Brooke looks over at me with wide eyes.

"I met her when I was in the hospital in Germany. Her brother is my team leader. *Was* my team leader. He was injured too, and his bed was next to mine. She hasn't left my side since."

95

"That's so sweet. Your kids and grandkids will sit starry eyed and listen to how you two fell in love." Brooke smiles.

"I don't know if she's there yet," I say honestly.

"But you are," Brooke says, and it's not a question.

"Yeah, one hundred percent I'm there."

"She's there, I can see it, but she might not realize it."

"I think she may not be willing to let herself admit it yet, and I understand why, too."

"Just give her time. She wouldn't be here every day like this if she didn't feel something."

"I have nothing but time," I say.

I'll wait her out. I'm good at waiting.

# Chapter 17

## Lexi

I can't believe I fell asleep and slept the whole night in a hospital bed, and it was the best sleep I've had in years. I can't stop myself from smiling all the way home. Once I'm home, I make a quick breakfast, shower, and change.

Just as I'm about to walk back out the door, I have a thought. I promised Noah home cooked food. He's been eating solid food and doesn't have many restrictions anymore.

So, I head into my kitchen and make him a bacon and cheese omelet with some breakfast potatoes. After placing them in a Tupperware container, I put it in my tote bag I've been bringing each day. I also grab a Gatorade for him, it's somewhat healthy, but it has a flavor, and he's only been drinking water.

When I get to Noah's room, I still have to pause and enjoy the sight of him. The normal clothes still throw me. Even though it's just a t-shirt and sweats, he's still hot as hell. Add in his face lighting up, when he sees me, and it's almost too much for my heart to take. I close the door behind me and smile.

"Everything okay?" He asks, a bit concerned.

"Well, I'm on a secret mission and don't want to get caught."

I wink at him.

With a twinkle in his eyes, he smiles, "Oh, yeah?"

I pull his rolling table over to him, open my bag, and take out the breakfast I made him, along with a fork and the Gatorade. When he sees the food, his whole face lights up again.

"I smuggled in food for you and a drink with some taste to it."

"Lexi." He says, choked up. "Come here." He holds out his hand.

I take it, and he pulls me in for a quick kiss.

"You're amazing, you know that?" He asks.

I wink at him. "Eat up, before we get caught."

He laughs and digs into the food.

"Oh, my God, bacon. I've missed bacon."

"I don't know what you like in your omelet, but I figured bacon was a safe bet."

"This is the best omelet I've ever had."

I wave my hand at him. "It could be the worst omelet, and you'd still say that because it's real eggs and not hospital food."

"No, I mean it, Lexi." He levels me with a serious stare.

I watch him eat it all, and it feels great to have someone other than my family to cook for again. When he's done, I clean up the evidence, and then he pats the bed next to him, so I go snuggle up with him. We put on some TV, and about an hour later, there's a knock on the door, and Becky peeks her head in.

"Can I borrow Lexi for lunch?"

"Everything okay?" I ask, instantly worried.

"Yes, I just want to talk to you." She says with a real smile, not a forced one, so I know it can't be too bad.

"Of course," I lean over to give Noah a kiss.

"Eat all your lunch, and I'll smuggle you something back," I tell him.

"Deal." He kisses me again, "Go have some girl talk."

I walk with Becky to the cafeteria, and we get our food. I pick out a loaded baked potato soup and some bread.

"This soup is surprisingly good," I say after my first bite. "But that's enough stalling, what's up?"

"Well, two things. First, I got the info for Noah's stuff and have help lined up for tomorrow." She sends me a text with the details, while she talks. "The guys will meet us there tomorrow morning at eight. They have trucks, and plus, with my car and your car, we should be able to do it in one trip." She says.

"You aren't lifting anything," I tell her.

"Johnny said the same thing, and I promised him, and I promise you, no lifting. I'm just offering up my SUV."

"Okay, I think I'm going to put his stuff in the empty bedroom in the basement. No one uses it, so it will be out of the way, but easy for him to assess if he needs anything."

"I agree."

"Okay, next on your agenda," I joke.

"So, one of the other wives put me in touch with a charity who helps bring families out to visit service members who are injured in action. It's through the USO. They cover the flights and hotel costs. I talked to them, and they're going to write a check for accommodations, even though they're staying with you. It's like they're renting rooms at an Airbnb." She says.

"I don't want the money."

"I figured, but the money for the flights and this check, plus the money we already raised, it's enough for them to come out here for a week. More than enough, but add this money, and they'll have a buffer."

It's a relief to know we did it. We're able to bring his family out here.

"So, I thought you'd like to do the honors and call them with the news since they will be your future in-laws and all." She says with a smile.

I gasp. "Becky, please don't."

She shrugs, "Okay, but we know where this is going, even if you don't."

"Not a word of this to Noah. I want to surprise him," I tell her.

"All right." She agrees.

I grab another meal of soup and bread to go and hide it in my bag.

"I do the same thing for Johnny." Becky laughs.

When I get up to Noah's room, I close the door again and pull out the soup and bread.

"It's pretty good, and what I had for lunch," I tell him.

As he eats, I fill him in on moving his stuff tomorrow morning.

"So, I won't be in, until about lunchtime," I tell him.

"You sure you have room?"

"Eight bedrooms, Noah. Eight. Yes, I have room."

We spend the rest of the day snuggling and watching TV before I head home and get ready to call Noah's parents.

Before dialing the number Becky gave me, I take a deep breath, and a female voice answers the phone.

"Hello, Mrs. Carr?" I ask.

"Yes?"

"My name is Lexi, and I'm a friend of Noah's," I say.

There's a ragged intake of breath on the other end of the line.

"How is my baby?" She asks almost near tears.

"He's doing great, I promise. He's a hero and really well liked. My brother is one of the guys Noah saved in the blast, and I will be forever grateful to him."

Shoot, that was the wrong thing to say because she starts crying hysterically before a man gets on the phone.

"Hello, who is this?" He asks.

"I'm sorry, Mr. Carr. My name is Lexi, and I'm a friend of Noah's. I didn't mean to make your wife cry," I tell him quickly.

"Is Noah okay?"

"Yes, he's fine, I promise. I was just telling your wife that my brother is one of the guys he saved in the blast. I didn't mean to upset her, and this is totally off topic of why I called. Sorry, I'm a bit nervous." I tell him.

"It's okay, any friend of Noah's is welcome around here." He says, his tone friendlier now.

"All right, let me take a more direct approach. Noah is really well liked in The Unit, and my brother knew he was sending money home each month, and things are tight. He said you weren't able to visit, so his wife and I took up a collection, along with the USO for your plane tickets for all four of you. You will be staying with me, as I have plenty of room. And there's money to supplement your lost income for the week off work."

Crap, now I made his dad cry, too. I don't do well, especially with guys crying.

"Are you serious?" He says.

"Yes."

"We can't impose."

"Mr. Carr, I have an eight bedroom plantation home I'm fixing up. I live here alone, so trust me, I'd enjoy the company.

101

The only details that are negotiable are the dates you can be out here." I tell him.

"We need to call our jobs and arrange everything."

"Of course. Call me back on this number day or night. This is my cell number." I tell him.

"We'll be in touch."

I didn't expect to hear back from them tonight, but he calls back two hours later, saying they can fly out on Monday. That's three days from now. They agree with me to not say anything and surprise Noah.

I get back to Becky with all the details.

"One more thing," Becky says.

"What's up?"

"Johnny is coming home tomorrow, so mandatory family dinner at your parent's place."

"I'll be there."

What a busy weekend ahead.

# Chapter 18

## Lexi

Noah didn't have near as much stuff, as we expected. We had too many guys and too many trucks, but they all came to help because they wanted to see my house. I guess, my brother has talked a lot about it.

So, after giving them the full tour, they unloaded and headed out.

"You love showing this place off," Becky says.

"Yeah, it has a unique history long before me, and it will be here long after me, if I do my job right," I tell her.

"Well, I'm going to go now."

"I'm going to shower and make some lunch to take with me, and then I'll be right behind you. See you at dinner tonight."

After a quick shower and making Noah and me some sandwiches, I go to the hospital.

"Hey, angel," Noah says, as soon as I'm walking in the door.

"Well, we got all your stuff moved, gave the guys a tour of the house, and I made lunch," I say, as I pull the sandwiches out.

"I'm jealous they got to see the house before me." He says.

"Well, as soon as you bust out of here you get the grand detailed tour." I wink at him. "Speaking of which, Johnny is getting released today, and my parents are demanding a family dinner, so I have to leave early tonight."

Noah looks disappointed. I get it. We already have a short day together, which is being cut short even more.

"You should go try to talk to Easton. If anyone can get through to him, it would be you." I tell him.

Easton has been on my mind for a while. I haven't met him yet, but with everything he's been through, I just wish there was a way to help him.

"Yeah, I think I'll do that. Now, come snuggle with me."

"Didn't sleep well?" I ask.

"No, the second I closed my eyes, the nightmares were there. I need my Lexi." He says as we cuddle in his bed.

"Well, close your eyes for a bit and take a nap. I'm right here."

"I don't want to miss my time with you." He mumbles already drowsy.

"I know, but I'll be back tomorrow. I'm not going anywhere, and you need sleep. I'm happy to lay with you any time."

It's not long before he drifts off to sleep. I take the opportunity to watch him, as he sleeps. He's relaxed around me, and I love that. His family will be here the day after tomorrow, and I wait can't to surprise him. I almost want to tell him now just to see the look on his face, but I'll wait. It will be better for him to be surprised.

His nap flies by, and almost as soon as he's awake, I have to go and meet with my parents.

"I promise to be here right as visiting hours start," I tell him.

"With breakfast?" He asks.

"With breakfast in hand."

I give him a chaste kiss, because anything more, and I'll be late to my parents' house.

The entire drive there, I try to think of what I want to tell my parents. Though, I should have known Johnny and his big mouth would have gotten to them ahead of me.

"Lexi dear, you're always the last one here. Now, get in here and tell us about your boyfriend. We're so mad we had to hear it from your brother." Mom says while she steers me towards the living room.

"He's not my boyfriend, Mom," I say, smacking Johnny upside the head, as I walk by. It wasn't that hard, but he acts like I almost threw him from his chair.

"I told them, but they won't listen," Becky says.

I sit down and find both my parents already staring at me.

"He's not my boyfriend. He's a friend, the first person I've been able to open up to in a long time, and I don't appreciate it being turned into family gossip. This has been hard on me, harder than any of you will ever know." I glare at my brother.

"I didn't come here to be tonight's family topic. If that's the case, I'll leave, and you can talk all you want and make up whatever stories suit you," I say and level my parents with a glare. I instantly know I was a bit too harsh, but if I back track now, they won't stop it. I can apologize later.

I had to have a talk with them a few months after Tyler died. Many times, I'd come over, and all they wanted to talk about was how I was doing, what I should be doing, and why I wasn't doing this. Finally, I put my foot down and said if it kept up, I would stop coming to dinner each week. I skipped the following week, and when I showed up again, things were back on track. So, they know I mean business.

"We're here to talk about Johnny, and I believe they have

some news to tell you." I switch the focus to them, and whether they were ready to tell my parents or not, Becky is pregnant. So, they'll be telling them tonight, because payback is a bitch, and my brother knows it.

"Thanks, sis." He grumbles.

"Maybe, you should keep your nose to yourself, and I wouldn't throw you under the bus," I tell him.

"I told you so." Becky singsongs with a smile on her face.

"Oh, so what do you have to tell us?" My mom shifts her attention to him.

My dad winks at me. He knows exactly what I did.

"Why do we tell her things?" My brother asks Becky.

"Because she's my best friend. You knew what you were getting into when you married me. Move on." Becky says laughing.

"Well, since my ex-sister let it out of the bag," Johnny says and looks at Becky, as they both smile big.

"You're going to be grandparents!" Becky shouts, and the room gets loud with squeals and hugs.

I just sit back and take it all in. For years, I was preparing for this moment. When they would announce they were pregnant, I'd have to fight back tears, because it was supposed to be me, and I would never have this.

As I sit here and watch my parents hug Becky and Johnny, and my mom fawn all over Becky, I don't feel any of that. I'm happy for them and excited for this brand-new life, and for what's to come. Noah gave this back to me. Without Noah, I know I'd be in a dark place today, instead of smiling and happy for them.

I get up and hug Becky and Johnny, and then turn to my dad and hold my phone. "I'll be right back," I say.

He nods, and I go out to the back porch and call Noah. Once I get through to his room, it only rings a few times, before he picks up.

"Noah," I say, a smile in my voice.

"You okay, angel? Aren't you supposed to be having dinner with your family?" He asks concerned.

"Yeah, I'm good. Johnny and Becky just told them they're pregnant, and I needed to get away from the baby talk and thank you."

"Thank me for what?"

"I was dreading this day for a while now. I thought I'd be thrown back to the memories of planning for a family, and I wouldn't be able to support them. Then, you show up, and I don't know, but it's bearable now. I was even able to smile for them."

"I'm glad. Where are you now?" He asks.

"On the back porch. I just wanted to hear your voice." I admit.

"Any time, and I will always be here." He says.

We talk a little bit more before I get off the phone and help with dinner. The first dinner Johnny has been back to in over six months since he left for deployment.

For the first time, the dinner table feels light and not like a piece is missing. I can look at the chair Tyler sat in and smile, instead of fighting off tears. I'm starting to heal, I know it, and as I always knew, it had to be on my own time.

The next battle ahead of me is Noah's family.

# Chapter 19

## Lexi

On Sunday, we did a lot of cuddling to make up for the shortened day on Saturday. It'd been hell trying to keep the secret, and I have been going back and forth about what I would say about being in late tomorrow.

"I'm going to be in later tomorrow around lunchtime. But Becky will be in because Johnny has a physical therapy appointment in the morning. So, she'll hang out with you. When Johnny gets finished with PT, he'll come, too." I tell him.

"Everything okay?" He asks.

This is where I didn't want to lie, but I can't quite tell the truth either.

"Yeah, I just have a meeting," I tell him, hoping he won't press for more details because this alone isn't a lie. I am meeting his parents at the airport. If he wants more details, then I'll be forced to lie, which I don't want to do.

"Okay." He kisses the top of my head, and we go back to watching TV.

When I get home that night, I know there's no way I'm getting any sleep, so I make sure their rooms are ready and clean like I have been doing each night for the last few days. I make sure there are towels in the bathrooms, and extra blankets if they need them. Finally, around midnight, I pass out, only to be up again the next morning, before my alarm and unable to go back to sleep.

In case I hit any traffic going into Savannah, I head to the airport early. But I don't, so it gives me time to walk around the airport, and this is one of my favorites. There's no mistaking you have flown into the south when you get here.

The visitor area is set up like one of the famous historic courtyards with brick paths and old southern like storefronts, a huge glass roof, and trees all over. There are benches and rocking chairs scattered around.

I'm really glad they're flying in here, and while I know their main focus is Noah, I hope they take a moment to enjoy the area, too. Once I know their plane lands, I'm waiting with a sign in my hands that says, *'Noah's Family.'* As soon as they see me, I have four people surrounding me in one huge hug. It's a bit overwhelming.

"Oh, look how pretty she is, Jim!" Noah's mother exclaims, who looks a lot like Aunt Becky from *Full House*.

"I apologize for my wife's manners. You can call me Jim, I'm Noah's father. This is my wife and Noah's mother, Janet, and Noah's sisters, Lucy and Grace." Noah's dad introduces everyone. He's a tall man with glasses, and the rough hands of a man, who works with his hands all day.

Noah's sisters look to be about high school age and are a bit shy. When I offer them a smile, they smile back, but I bet they're nervous about seeing their brother.

"Well, I'm Lexi. My brother is Noah's Team Leader and a pain in my rear end." I wink at Lucy and Grace, and that earns me a giggle.

"So, do you want to drop your stuff off and get settled or go right to the hospital?"

"Hospital," they all four say at once.

"I figured. Let's grab some lunch on the way, and I'll bring some food in for Noah. I've been sneaking him nonhospital food here and there when I can." I tell them.

We walk out to my car, and their eyes take in everything around them, but they don't slow down. I know they won't be okay, until they have eyes on Noah, and I can't blame them.

We grab some sandwiches from the local deli, before heading into the hospital.

"Give me just a minute," I say after we park.

I shoot off a quick text to Becky.

**Me:** Hey, we're here. Are we good to come up?

**Becky:** Yep, he just finished lunch, though he didn't eat much.

When I put my phone away, Janet places her hand on my shoulder, "What should we expect?" She asks.

I turn in my seat, so I can look at her in the back seat with Lucy and Grace.

"Well, you know the basics of what happened. He hasn't told me much more. The right side of his body has some burns. Most are hidden under his clothes, except for the ones on his neck and face. Part of his ear is gone, but his eye is fine and really, I've seen a lot worse. He'll be going in for plastic surgery to smooth out the scars."

I remember the first time I saw him with his bandages off. "It'll be jarring to see him the first time. Just be genuine with

110

your emotions and reactions. When you fake it, it will make us all uncomfortable." I say.

They all nod.

"Okay, my brother and his wife are hanging out with him now and have been keeping him company all morning," I say, as we make our way into the hospital and to the elevator. As we approach his room, I turn to them.

"He has no idea you're coming. Let me go in first, and then we'll bring you in as a surprise," I say, and again, they nod.

When I walk in, Noah's whole face lights up. "Hey, angel. Come sit with me."

"Well, I have two surprises for you. First, I brought you lunch." I pull out the sandwich for him.

"Perfect, I'm suddenly starving. But what's the second one?" Becky and Johnny move to the far side of the room, and Becky nods at the door, telling Noah's family to come in.

As Noah's parents walk in followed by his sisters, his eyes go wide.

"How…" Is all he gets out, before his mom and dad are hugging him, and all three are crying.

His sisters hang back a little and just watch.

"It was all this girl." His dad points to me, and Noah's eyes shoot to me.

I shake my head. "Becky did the leg work."

"But it was her idea," Becky says. "The USO paid for the plane tickets, and The Unit helped raise money to cover lost income. They're staying with Lexi, so it's all covered."

He doesn't get a chance to say anything before he sees his sisters, who are both frozen at the foot of his bed, unsure of what to do. So, I walk over and stand behind them.

"He's still the same guy. God just made him more badass

111

with some scars," I whisper, and they giggle, before running over to hug him, too.

His eyes lock with mine, and he mouths *'thank you.'* I smile and nod my head.

"Well, PT kicked my ass, so we're going home," Johnny says, and after some hugs, he and Becky head out.

Noah eats, while his parents start asking question after question. His mother starts fussing over him with tears in her eyes, and I start to feel like I'm intruding on family time.

"Well, I'm going to go…" I start to say.

"No, stay with me, angel." Noah stops me, and my cheeks heat at the nickname.

"Spend some time with your family, Noah." I wave him off. "I'll be back at dinner time."

"Lexi, please?" Noah says.

"Please, stay." His mom says. "We want to get to know you, too."

I look at his dad who nods as do his sisters.

"Okay," I start to go and sit on the couch.

"Angel…" Noah says in a warning tone and pats the bed next to him.

"So damn bossy," I grunt but walk over and sit on the edge of the bed down by his legs.

"Damnit, Lexi. Just because they're here changes nothing, and if I didn't think you'd run scared, I'd introduce you as my girlfriend."

My eyes go wide, and I can't speak to save my life.

"Yeah, I'm not playing around, and I'm not missing my Lexi time." He holds his hand out again, and this time I take it, and he pulls me into his side and wraps his arm around me like he's afraid I'll try to bolt.

"So, let's just be honest here." His mom says. "What happened to Whitney?"

"What a fucking bitch." I growl.

Then, realizing I said that out loud, I slap my hand over my mouth.

Noah just laughs. "She'll have to tell you the story. I was pretty out of it."

So, I recap our first day in Germany for them, and they just keep shaking their heads.

"We never liked her anyway, and she was always mean to us." Lucy, the oldest, says.

Noah shakes his head, "I'm sorry I should have paid more attention."

"We could tell you weren't in love with her, and we were hoping you'd figure it out on your own." His mom says. "But you two." She looks between us. "It warms my heart."

My cheeks flush again, and I look down at my lap, as Noah tightens his arm around me.

"Mom, don't scare her off. I just got her to admit she likes me, and I'm still working on the girlfriend title," Noah says.

I shake my head, and thankfully, his dad changes the subject to people back home, until Noah starts to yawn. It's almost 3 p.m., and Noah always naps after lunch.

"Want us to let you rest?" I ask.

"No, I want to nap with you," he mumbles.

I look at his parents, and that comment didn't go unnoticed.

"He's been trying to take himself off his sleep medicine, and in doing so, it brought back the nightmares," I tell them.

"But when I lay down with her, she keeps the nightmares away." He says, snuggling up to my side.

"I'm sure your parents want to get settled in," I say, trying to

113

sit up.

He pulls me back down. "Call Becky," he whispers.

"I'm sorry," I laugh, as I apologize to his parents.

"It's perfectly okay." His mom says.

I call Becky, and she's back twenty minutes later to take his parents to my house.

"Make sure you give them a house tour, please, or else they'll get lost. I thought his parents could take the yellow room at the end of the hallway. Then, the girls could take the room with the Jack and Jill bath. They can share a room, or each can have their own, it's up to them."

"I'll give them the grand tour, don't worry," Becky says.

"Make yourself at home, and you're free to roam. Any part of the history can be found online just search Oakside Plantation. You can show them the unfinished room in the basement, but that's the only room I ask you don't go in. I don't know how safe it is."

"Oh, and there's lasagna in the fridge for you. Cook it at 350 degrees for 45 minutes, and also, I figured while you're here, you can use Noah's truck, because it needs to be driven. Becky, you know where the keys are."

"Okay, see you soon." They say and head out of the door.

I lay down facing Noah, and he's on his side, looking at me. He brings his hand to my face and cups my cheek.

"Best thing someone has ever done for me." He says with a smile. "You have no idea what it means to have them here." He leans in and kisses me. "Be my girlfriend, Lexi, because I'm head over heels in love with you, and I know this isn't a traditional relationship."

"I don't care about that," I tell him.

"Just so you know angel, even if you say no, you're still mine, and I'm not letting you go."

What girl doesn't want to hear someone wants them so bad they don't care if you say no? That's the dream, right?

I lean in and kiss him softly. "I'll be your girlfriend," I tell him, and his smile is blinding.

"The other part just be patient with me, okay?"

"Always, angel, always."

I reach up and trace the scars on his face; I have them memorized by now.

"So, what special privileges come with the girlfriend status?" I ask, joking around.

"Extra kisses." He leans in and kisses me, giving my bottom lip a light nip.

"So far, so good."

"Name anything, and it's yours, angel."

I don't say a word. I just rest my hand on his hip, and then slowly work it under his shirt.

"Angel…"

"Don't hide from me, Noah. I want all of you, including the scars."

He closes his eyes and lets me feel his scars. I slide my hands up his side, over his chest to his shoulder, and then slowly back down. His whole body shutters, when I move back down over his ribs.

"Nap with me, angel." He says as we snuggle up together. Before I know it, we're both asleep.

# Chapter 20

**Lexi**

I wake up to giggles, filling the room. Opening my eyes, I find his family is back.

"Mom totally got a picture of you two," Grace says.

I smile, "Will you send it to me?" I ask.

His mom nods, and I slowly slip out of bed, careful not to wake him.

"Is that house really yours?" Lucy asks in an excited whisper.

"Yeah, it's my dream house. It needs a lot of love still, but it keeps me busy." I tell them.

"It's really gorgeous." His mom says.

Noah starts to whimper in his sleep, so I sit back down on the bed and rub his back. No one says a word, as I lie back down and start calling his name, trying to gently wake him.

"Go back to sleep, angel." He says without opening his eyes.

"Noah, wake up."

"No sleep."

I laugh. "Your parents are back."

He groans but sits up and tries to get his bearings.

"They brought dinner, while you slept. You need to eat." I

tell him.

While he eats, his family talks about the house, and Noah listens just shakes his head.

"I'm jealous you got to see it before I did," Noah says.

"Well, there's your incentive to get out of here," I tell him.

"It would make a killer bed-and-breakfast," Lucy interjects.

"I don't know if I could handle losing my privacy like that all the time," I tell her. "I believe as I fix her up, she will show me the journey she's supposed to take next."

"Do you know any of the history of the place?" His dad asks.

"There was a fire that destroyed a lot of buildings on the property and part of the house during the Civil War. It used to be over 3,000 acres, but most of it was sold off, and I now own fifty acres with the house. There are a few small buildings scattered around, but they all need to be repaired." I say.

"Well, I have some good news," Noah interrupts. "I want to officially introduce you to my girlfriend." Noah beams.

His family cheers, and I know I'm blushing. We sit and chat, until visiting hours are up, and then we all head to my home.

When we get back to the house, Lucy asks about my photo set up.

"Well, this is supposed to be the grand dining room, but I don't have a lot of people over, so I set it up to do photos," I tell her.

"What kind of photos? I love photography. Noah even bought me my own camera last year for Christmas." Lucy says.

"Mostly food. I run a food website, and I'm working on a cookbook."

"Oh, I love to cook!" Grace says.

"And she is really good, too. No one knows where she got it

from, because it sure wasn't me." Noah's mom says.

"Well, I need to do a photo shoot tomorrow, before we head in, so you want to help me? You know, if it's something you guys are interested in, I'm always looking for help. If Grace wants to cook and you do photos, I pay one hundred dollars a recipe, and plus, I pay for the food to make the recipes.

The girls decide to go to bed, but his parents stay up to chat with me.

"Do you mind if we talk a bit?" Jim says.

"Is this a stiff drink kind of talk?" I joke, as we head to the living room and sit down.

"No, no." He says, but I offer them both a drink anyway, and they take me up on it.

"How is he really?" Jim asks.

"He's good. There was a lot of waiting for the bandages to come off, and I could tell he was nervous about it, but once they came off, he was able to start some small PT, and he's excited to be moving forward. He talks to the plastic surgeon later this week, mostly to help fix his ear. Though, he hears fine, it's just aesthetics. I'm not sure what else they'll do, but it will mostly be on his neck and face."

They nod, so I continue.

"He took himself off the sleep medication and the painkillers, and now, he only takes them, when he really needs them. As far as I know, he hasn't used either in about a week. Sleeping at night is now his biggest battle. I've fallen asleep there before, and the nurses would rather he sleep than have the nightmares, so they don't wake us up."

They go on to ask about our time in Germany, and I give them every detail I can remember, and how Noah was.

"The girls are excited to work with you. They said you

offered them a job?"

"Yes, with me spending all my time with Noah, I haven't been able to photograph recipes like I'd like. If they're able to do it, when you get back home, then it will free up some time for me to work on the house. Plus, then you guys will have some food to eat for a while. I can only eat so many leftovers." I laugh.

"Well, we appreciate it, even one or two a month will be a help," Janet says.

"Oh, I was thinking more like one or two a week," I say, and their eyes go wide.

Janet tears up. "You have been such a blessing in such a short amount of time."

"I don't want to pry, but I know what it's like to live paycheck to paycheck and struggle. I didn't have kids, though. I know you have family back home, but if things get bad, you're always welcome here. All I ask is for help cleaning. God, I love this place, but hate cleaning it." I say, and they laugh.

"Things have been okay. We have four more years, and then, we'll own our home. Times have been hard, but we always find a way to make it work." Jim says.

"Your websites really make enough to pay for this place?" Janet asks, as her eyes roam the living room with most of its original details.

I look down at my hand in my lap, as my eyes prick with tears. I was hoping to avoid this subject, but somehow, I knew we wouldn't be able, too.

"I'm sorry Janet doesn't think sometimes," Jim says.

"No, I have nothing to hide." I stand up and walk over to the fireplace behind them and touch Tyler's shadow box with this folded flag and medals. When Janet sees it, she gasps.

119

"I was married to a Marine. The most amazing, sweetest man. This place was my dream. On his second deployment, his unit was hit with an IED, and he didn't survive the flight to Germany. I didn't know he had taken a life insurance policy out besides what the military pays. It was more than enough to buy this place. My websites pay for my bills and some extra. I've been slowly renovating." I say, looking around.

"How long ago?" Janet asks.

"Four years now. I never planned to marry again, as he was my soul mate. But recently, I was reminded of a promise I made him. To live and find love again. He didn't want me to be alone. When I was feeling guilty about how I felt about Noah, Tyler made me remember."

I stare at the photos on the mantle. One of us on our wedding day. Us and Becky at Johnny's wedding. His boot camp graduation. And one the morning he was leaving for deployment. The last time I ever saw him alive.

"I'm so sorry," Janet says, coming over to hug me.

"Noah saved me more than he knows. He's helped me to move on and live again. For that, I will always be grateful." I tell them.

# Chapter 21

**Noah**

My family has been here for a few days, and it's great to catch up with them. My mom is constantly fussing over me, and my dad doesn't seem to know what to do with himself with all this time off work, but he's here and making the best of it.

Even so, when they walk in today, my eyes go right to Lexi.

"Hey, angel," I say, as she leans down to give me a kiss on the cheek.

"I have to go for a bit. Becky has her first doctor's appointment, and they asked me to be there. So, I'm going to leave you with your family and be back later. I'll sneak you some food." She winks at me.

I hold her hand, "Call me if it gets too much, okay?"

I know this pregnancy has been hard for her, and she keeps saying she's taking it so much better than she expected, because of me, but I know it's still hard. Every now and then, I see it in her eyes.

She wants to be there for her brother and her best friend, and she'll do anything for them, even if it means locking her emotions away, but I don't want her to do that with me.

"I promise." She smiles and leans in for a quick kiss.

I wrap my hand behind her head and really kiss her. Though, she doesn't hesitate to kiss me back, but she pulls away much sooner than I'd like. Apparently, she's still shy about kissing and snuggling with me in front of my parents.

On the way out, she hugs my parents and my sisters, and I watch her go. This will be the first time I'm alone with my family, since they've been here, and I want to use this time to talk to them. I want to know how they feel about Lexi because I don't want to make the same mistake as I did with Whitney.

"She's special, that girl." My dad says with a smile on his face.

"Yeah?" I encourage him.

"We have spent the nights talking with her, and she's been through so much. She isn't afraid of hard work, and she's so good with your sisters."

"Guess what! Lexi is showing us how she photographs her recipes and is going to pay us to create some for her website. This morning she let me photograph breakfast!" Lucy squeals.

"What do you mean she's going to pay you for recipes?" I ask.

"Oh, she said being here with you she's gotten behind, and once you're out she wants to free up some time to work on the house. So, she'll pay us to cook and photograph some recipes. One hundred dollars each, plus, she buys the food." Grace says.

"It's true. Lexi was telling us she would need one or two a week," Dad says, while he looks out of the window.

I get choked up because I've been worried about my parents missing the money I've been sending home to them each month, but having this extra income, will help offset a little of that.

"We really like her. She's nice and even showed me a few tricks on the camera." Lucy says.

"She's great with them." My mom adds. "And she's a good cook."

"Yeah, that I knew, because she's been sneaking me food. I can only take so much hospital food," I say.

"Any idea how much longer you'll be here?" My dad asks.

"Ahhh, I have an operation coming up with the plastic surgeon. He wants to do it, while the scars are still new because they'll be easier to work with. When someone is talking about working on my face, I zone out. It kind of creeps me out. After that, they move me to a rehabilitation section to work with a physical therapist and physiologist, and once I can take care of myself, they release me." I tell them.

"What are your plans, then?" Dad asks.

I take a deep breath. "I don't really know. The paperwork has started for my VA disability, so I have that. Since I'll I have the GI Bill, I was thinking of going back to school. They'll pay for it and give me living expenses. I'm not sure what I want to go back to school for, though."

"Well, you know you can move home and stay with us and go to school. We'd be happy to have you." Mom says.

"I know Mom, but..." I can't bring myself to say it.

"You want to stay here and see if things work out with that pretty lady of yours." She finishes for me.

"Yeah," I say.

Mom nods, "I figured. You seem to have a good support system here, too."

"I'd like to be here, when the guys get home, too."

"Well, what are you thinking for school?" My dad chimes in.

"I'm not sure. Business maybe. I know with that kind of a

general degree, it gives me a lot of options. I thought about teaching, but I don't want to sit in front of a group of people, looking like this. What I keep leaning more and more too, is helping out other injured veterans. Just need to figure out how."

"Maybe, a counselor or social worker to help them transition?" My mom says.

"Could be. I still need to think it through some more. Maybe, do some research." I tell them.

"How have you been sleeping?" Mom asks.

"Still having nightmares, but they aren't as bad as the first few nights."

"Lexi still helping?" Mom asks.

"Yeah. I feel safe with her like she has my back no matter what. I think that's a big part of it. The doctor says they should eventually go away if I work through it, so I'm trying."

"What happened?" My dad asks.

When I look at him and then look at my sisters, he seems to understand and just nods.

"Why don't you girls go and find us some lunch?" Dad says, pulling out his wallet and giving them some money.

Lucy looks at him; she knows my dad is trying to get rid of them for this conversation, but finally gives in and takes the money in one hand, and Grace's hand in the other. Before I begin, I make sure they're out of the door.

"We were on patrol when the IED went off. I don't remember much, but Moore's leg was under some debris in front of me, and I went to get him. I felt the heat on my right side from the fire, but I didn't feel the fire. Then, I got him out, and that's about all I remember. I guess, getting him free saved two others as well from what they're telling me. I have a brief moment of waking up on the ride to Germany, but they knocked me right back out. The next time I woke up, there was Whitney and Lexi in the room with me. After that, I was in and out of it. Then, for the plane ride from Germany, they kept me sedated, and when I didn't wake up for three days, it upset Lexi."

"We always knew this was a possibility. That doesn't mean the phone call was any easier to get." Dad whispers.

"I know, and I'm sorry I worried you."

"Oh, you're here and alive, and that's all that matters. Plus, you got to meet Lexi. If you had to go through all this to find her, would you really change any of it?" Mom asks.

I turn my head and look out of the window. This hasn't been easy; it's been the most painful and difficult thing I've ever been through. But Lexi? She's the most amazing person I've ever met. Could I imagine not having her in my life? If none of this had happened, I'd still be with Whitney, and I know that's not where I want my life to take me.

"I wouldn't change a thing," I say.

# Chapter 22

## Lexi

The day after his family leaves, we're snuggling in his hospital bed watching TV. I have my back to his chest and his hand has been rubbing the skin on my hip and driving me crazy.

"Lexi, I need to talk to you about something."

"Okay," I start to turn to face him, but he stops me.

"This will be easier for me to say if you aren't looking at me." When he says that, I'm worried.

"Everything okay?" I ask.

"I was so excited that you agreed to be my girlfriend that I wasn't thinking it through, and I didn't want to have this conversation in front of my parents."

Crap, I've screwed this up already, and he's breaking up with me. Stupid me for putting my heart on the line.

"I'm not breaking up with you." He says into my ear like he can read my mind. "I left out some details the doctor told me."

"Noah, what's wrong?" I ask my heart racing now. Either he's breaking up with me, or something's wrong. Whichever way it is, I don't think this is going to be a good conversation.

"The doctor said due to the burns and the scarring locations he wasn't sure if... um, well, if I will be able to have kids or..." he trails off.

I take his hand in mine that's on my hip, and then pull it around me. His scarred hand that he lets only me touch. I bring it to my lips and kiss that beautiful scarred hand that saved lives. Kids aren't a deal breaker for me. Hell, for a while, I've had it in my head that I'd never have kids. Yet, I feel like there's something else.

"No secrets, Noah,"

He buries his head in the back of my neck and kisses my shoulder.

"He doesn't know if I'll be able to have kids or even... perform."

"Perform?" I ask, a bit lost.

"Get hard again." He whispers.

"Oh," I say, letting that sink in.

"I know kids are your dream, so I understand if you don't want to be with me, as it's asking you to give up a lot."

This time I don't let him stop me from turning around. I take his face with both my hands.

"Noah, stop," he takes a shaky breath, but he still won't meet my eyes.

"This isn't a deal breaker for me."

Finally, he meets my eyes, and I see the question there.

"It's not?"

"Noah... dreams change. I haven't had hope of having kids for years now. Even since I met you, I haven't thought about it outside of Becky being pregnant. Once I thought about a sperm donor, but then decided I didn't want to do it on my own. There's always adoption. I have a huge house to fill and so many kids who need a home." I tell him.

He still isn't convinced, and I'm not going to drop this until he is.

"Noah?" I ask, trying to pull it out of him.

"What if we can never have sex?" He mumbles.

I smirk because I like it that sex with me is on his mind, because it has been on my mind, too.

"Well, would you be selfish about it?"

"No. I'd make sure you were taken care of daily. Multiple times a day."

Lord, if that isn't a turn on! The sexy man in front of me wanting to give me orgasms multiple times a day. My mind races as I wonder what are the chances of him getting started now.

But when he swallows hard and opens his mouth, I never expect what comes out of it.

"You could, uh… always find someone…" He starts.

"Noah," I growl. "An open marriage or relationship is a deal breaker for me. Your hands work and so does your mouth."

To prove the point, he leans in and kisses me. It's raw and needy, leaving me breathless.

When he pulls back, I can't help but smile. "Yes, your mouth is perfect," I say in a freshly kissed daze.

"I don't see a problem here, Noah."

He closes his eyes, takes a deep breath, and smiles. "How did I get so damn lucky?"

"Same way I did," I say, kissing him again.

Wrapping his arm around my waist, he pulls me in close and deepens the kiss. I run my hands through his hair.

"So, have you tried?" I ask against his lips.

"Tried to what?" He asks, his kisses gliding down my neck.

"To get hard."

He pulls back and sighs. "No."

"Can we try?"

"God, only a crazy man would say no to that, angel." With a smile, I get up and lock the door.

"Maybe, a little visual?" I take my top off, leaving me in my shorts and a bra.

"Fuck, you're sexy." He says as he watches me walk back over him. I maneuver on the bed, so he's lying back a bit more, but still sitting up enough to watch. His eyes follow my every move, as I climb in the bed with him and lean over to kiss him.

Kissing him, I trail my hand lightly down his chest and across his hips, and then over his cock, making his body still.

"Baby, you've got to relax," I say, moving my hand.

"I'm scared." He whispers.

"It's all right if it doesn't happen. We'll try again," I kiss him. "And again." Kiss. "And again. And we'll have fun trying, okay? This should be fun, and if it's not, we're doing something wrong."

"Okay," he nods.

"Then, lay back and let me take care of you." Eager to begin, I lay down next to him.

He pushes my bra to one side and runs his thumb over the stiff peaks of my nipples. "You deserve so much better than a hospital room." He growls.

"Yet, I don't remember the last time I've been so turned on."

His eyes travel up and meet mine, as his hand moves down to the edge of my shorts and pushes them to the side. He runs a finger over my panties.

"Fuck, you're soaked, angel." He groans.

"Told you," I smirk.

I turn to the side and move my hand to his pants. As I reach into his pants and give his cock a tug, he twitches, so I play with him, and he starts breathing hard.

"You okay?"

"Yeah, it feels good, but…"

But he's still soft. I give him a few more strokes, and he groans and pulls me up the bed to kiss me. "We'll just have to keep trying," I say.

He kisses down my belly and unbuttons my shorts.

"Noah, you don't have, too," I say.

He kisses me just below my belly button.

"I meant it, Lexi. I'll always take care of you." He says and pulls my shorts down.

He kisses my clit over my panties, and I throw my head back with a groan. Then, pulling my panties to the side, he runs his finger through my slick folds.

"You're so wet, angel." I moan.

"That's what you do to me, baby," I tell him.

"So damn sexy." He says as he thrusts a finger into me, and I have to hold my hand over my mouth to stop the moan. "And so damn tight." He says as he adds a second finger in me. He slowly thrusts them in and out, using his thumb to stoke my clit. My hips buck, wanting him closer, so he increases the pressure on my clit, and I start cumming so hard that I have to grab the pillow and bury my face in it. I was never one to be loud, but I don't think I've ever been this turned on either.

He lazily moves his finger in and out of me, until I start to relax. When he pulls his finger out, he licks them clean and then helps me put my shorts back on. He presses his warm lips to my stomach and drops tiny kisses, before stopping and looking into my eyes. The intensity between us is electrifying. When he runs his hand over my breast again, I shiver, because

I'm still sensitive from my orgasm.

"Thank you, angel. Watching you let go like that, is a gift I'll never forget." He says, kissing me tenderly.

When he pulls back, I groan, but sit up and put my shirt back on and readjust my clothes, before going back to the door, unlocking and cracking it open. Then, I go lay back down with him and snuggle up to his side.

"You're very comfy."

"Get some sleep, angel."

"You too," I mumble, as I close my eyes.

# Chapter 23

### Noah

Today, is the day I talk to the plastic surgeon and to say I'm nervous is an understatement. It's one thing to have emergency surgery because you have to, but choosing to go under the knife like this, is much scarier.

I'm sitting on the couch with Lexi snuggled up to my side. It's been great being able to move around my room a bit, even if I still need help to do so.

"Hello, Noah. I'm Dr. Taylor. I'll be your plastic surgeon. I consulted with your doctor, and he said we were just going to focus on your face and neck?" He launches right into it after shaking my hand.

"Yeah," I say, as Lexi stands up, and I grab her hand.

"I'm not going far, Noah. I'm just going to sit on the bed, so I'm not in his way," Lexi says smiling.

Dr. Taylor sits and examines my ear and my face, which makes me uncomfortable. The whole time Lexi holds my eyes and concentrating on her, makes it bearable. The doctor explains what he'll be doing and several times when he mentioned peeling the skin back Lexi cringed, and I can't blame her.

"So, I know that was a lot of medical jargon, but in short we will use some skin grafts to smooth out the scarring on your neck and cheek. We will rebuild some of your cheekbone and reconstruct your ear. Because your ear is more for aesthetics, it will be the last surgery we do. I think we can do all this in six surgeries with a week or two in between each one, maybe less, depending on how they heal. Any questions for me?"

My mind goes blank, but Lexi is right there.

"What kind of PT can he do if any? He hasn't started, but they want to get him moving on it."

"Light muscle work where he stays in bed is all. He'll be able to move around his room as he feels up to it, but that's about it." The doctor says.

Lexi comes back to sit next to me, as the doctor talks a bit more about the procedures and aftercare. He again asks if there are any questions. Lexi is silent, so I squeeze her hand.

"Sorry, I zoned out a little. It's hard to focus when he's talking about cutting you open and stitching you back up."

"He was asking if this is still something I want to do."

"This choice is yours, Noah. You're the one who will be in pain. I will always support whatever choice you make, but for the record, I love you just the way you are."

Holy shit, did she just say she loves me? All I can think about now is getting this doctor out of here as fast as possible.

"I'll do them," I say.

"Great," the doctor says. "The skin grafts we did last week are looking good, so we'll reach out with a surgery date in a few days." Then, he says goodbye and leaves the room.

My eyes are still locked on Lexi, as I pull her into my lap.

"Say it again, angel."

"Say what?"

"You said you loved me," I whisper.

She smiles, leaning in to give me a soft kiss.

"I love you, Noah. With everything I am, I love you." Her words fail me, my heart is beating fast, and all I see is her.

Pouring my emotions into a kiss, I want to say without words what she means to me.

"I love you too, Lexi. That's why I'm choosing to do the surgeries."

"I don't get it?" She says with a frown.

"You deserve more than being out to dinner with the biggest freak in the room."

"Damnit, Noah. You are not a freak, and anyone who dares to say so will end up with worse scars than you." She says angrily.

She reaches up to trace my scars, so I close my eyes and just feel.

"You know I have every line," she leans in and kisses the scars by my eye. "Every dip," she starts kissing down my face. "Every twist," she places kisses along my jaw. "And turn of these scars memorized." She kisses the corner of my mouth. My whole body shutters, feeling her soft lips on my rough skin.

"Will you take a picture with me?"

I nod, and she pulls up her phone, turns my head, so the scars are facing the camera, and I'm looking at her.

"You tend to hide your scars when others are around, but I want to remember them, Noah. I don't want you to hide around me or anyone, but I want to remember you just like this." She says.

For her, I'll take the photo with my scars on full display, as uncomfortable as it makes me. For her, I would do anything.

"Promise me, you won't hide from me." She whispers as she goes back to kissing my scars.

Each kiss is turning me on a little more.

"I promise."

The more she kisses me, the more kisses I want. My body hums with electricity, and I feel like I can do anything, so long as she keeps kissing me.

Then, I take her hand and place it over my cock. It's not much, but it's a semi and better than it has been when we've tried before.

She kisses back up to my good ear. "See, it's getting better every time." Then, she gets up and locks the door.

When she comes back to me, she falls to her knees between my legs.

"Lexi…" I whisper.

She smiles and pulls my shirt up and traces the scars on my side and ribs. Then, she leans in and kisses down to the waistband of my pants. She looks up at me, as her hands slowly move the waistband of my sweatpants, and then with slow deliberate moves, she pulls them down to pull my cock out.

My nerves start to get to me again, and I try to put them away and just concentrate on her hand on me. The sensations of her touching me. When she strokes my cock, there's a twitch, but nothing else. My eyes are still closed, and suddenly, I feel her mouth on me.

My eyes pop open, and it's erotic, watching her taking me into her mouth. Though, my heart starts racing along with my mind, nothing happens. I can't take disappointing her anymore, so I'm grateful when she tilts her head to look up at me and tucks my cock back into my pants.

"Your turn, angel," I say, as I pull her back up to me. She straddles my lap and settles with her arms around my neck.

"It will just take time, Noah. You'll see." She says, kissing me again.

While she kisses me, I run my hand up her thighs to the edge of her shorts and run my thumbs along the edge for a moment, before pulling them to the side and rubbing over her lace panties.

"I love how you're always wet for me," I tell her.

I still can't believe she gets turned on by my scars. That the ugly skin does this to her.

"Will I still turn you on, when the scars are gone?" I ask as the question flashes through my head.

She frames my face with both hands and tilts my head to look at her.

"Oh, Noah. What turns me on is you. How sweet you are, how much you love me, how much I love you, and how brave you are. Your scars are a part of you, and that's why I like them. But even when they're gone or mostly gone, you will still turn me on. I think my body is conditioned to get excited as soon as you say angel now." Deciding to put that to the test, I push her panties aside and run my fingers through her folds.

"Is that so, angel?" I ask, and sure enough, she gets wetter.

As I thrust two fingers into her and start playing with her clit in the way I know drives her crazy, she starts riding my hand. I can tell you there's nothing as sexy as seeing how turned on she is by me, as her eyes sparkle and her cheeks flush.

"Noah…" She whispers my name before her mouth crashes into mine. With her tongue tangling with mine, her hands in my hair, and her riding my fingers, it's all almost too much. The sensations are overwhelming.

When her walls start to clamp down on my finger, I know she's close. She grinds down harder and then starts cumming. I use my free hand to pull her in for a hard kiss and swallow her moans until she relaxes and collapses against my chest.

I pull my finger from her and lick them clean. I'm addicted to the taste of her, sweet and tangy.

I hold her to me. Yes, for this girl, I'd do just about anything.

# Chapter 24

**Lexi**

Today, I'm at the hospital at an ungodly hour. The sun is barely up, and they're prepping Noah for his first surgery. To say I'm nervous wouldn't even begin to cover how I'm feeling.

He seems remarkably calm for someone getting ready to go under the knife, but he has also spent the morning telling anyone who will listen he wants me in his recovery room when he wakes up. He's been told multiple times it's on his chart, but he still makes sure.

In a way, it's comforting to know he wants me there that much.

"Noah, I promise, I'll be there," I say, after he tells his nurse, Brooke, again for the third time in an hour. Thankfully, she just laughs and smiles.

A nurse in green scrubs and a bandanna in her hair knocks on the door.

"Okay, Mr. Carr, it's time." She smiles.

The grip Noah has on my hand tightens, and he pulls me in for a kiss. This kiss is soft, sweet, and full of promise, leaving me breathless. When I pull back, I rest my forehead on his and run my hand over his scars one last time.

"I love you, angel. I'll see you soon."

"I love you too, Noah. Fight your way back to me."

"Always, angel, always." He says before I step back and watch them wheel him out. I make my way to the surgery waiting room to find Johnny, Becky, Mom, and Dad, waiting on me with breakfast and coffee.

I sit down to eat, and just as I'm finishing, his mom calls.

"I'm on my way to work, but wanted to check in."

"They just took him back, and there's nothing to report yet."

"Okay, well call me soon as you do, no matter what, okay?"

"I promise," I say and hang up.

I start pacing the room and know I need a distraction, so I sit down next to Becky.

"Have you guys picked out baby names yet?" I ask them.

"No, we don't even know what we are having yet." Becky laughs.

"Great, let's pick out some names," I say, pulling out my phone and looking up baby name lists.

"I love you, sis, but you don't get a say in this," Johnny says.

"Humor me," I tell him, and he nods, understanding it's a distraction.

We start with girls' names, and they actually agree on a few and add them to their list. We laugh at some of them.

"Did a movie star really name their kid Banjo?" Becky asks.

"I really hope they were high. The poor kid."

"At least, once they're eighteen, they can file for a name change." My mom says, shaking her head.

Before I know it, the doctor comes out.

"Lexi?" He asks.

I jump up. "Yes?"

"Everything went well. It was a textbook surgery. He's getting transported to recovery now, and the nurse will be out soon to get you."

I call his mom and relay what the doctor said, and then I start pacing the waiting room.

"Do you want some lunch?" My dad asks.

"I couldn't eat if I tried."

"Why don't you sit down?" My mom pats the chair next to her.

I just shake my head.

About twenty minutes later, the nurse who took him to surgery comes out.

"Lexi, right this way." She smiles, as I hug Mom, Dad, Becky, and Johnny. I promise to call them with updates and agree to let them bring me dinner later before I follow the nurse back.

I enter a large room with beds lining the walls, all separated by curtains and a nurse's desk on the opposite wall facing the beds. It's set up a lot like the hospital in Germany.

"He'll be in and out of it, as he comes out of the anesthesia. Then, he'll be groggy with the pain medicine he's on." The nurse says.

Sighing, I nod, "Not our first rodeo with the pain medicine haze."

I sit in the chair next to his bed. Thankfully, it's on his left side, so I take his hand in mine and start talking to him. More for my benefit than his. I tell him that I called his mom, and then tell him about our baby name conversation in the waiting room.

Then, I move on to talking about my house.

"I've been trying to decide on wall colors for the house. I want to keep it natural and close to what would have been

140

there when the house was built, but they used wallpaper, and from what I'm finding, when I peel off some of the wallpaper, what they have used is horrible. But I'm thinking my next project will be to put a garden in. Something with a water feature, maybe some herbs. Every summer I think of putting in a pool because it gets so hot here." I say, lost in thought.

"Pools are a lot of fucking work," Noah croaks, his voice groggy and scratchy.

"Hey there, sexy." I smile.

"Angel." He groans.

"What do you need?"

"Water."

I hold the straw to his lips, as he drinks. Then, he leans back and looks at me. He starts to smile, and then groans.

"Fuck, that hurts."

"Anesthesia makes you cuss like a sailor." I joke.

"Not a sailor, a Marine." He grunts.

I laugh and lean in to kiss the cheek that isn't bandaged. I then go on to repeat everything I told him, while he was still out about his mom and the baby names.

I shoot off a text to his parents that he's awake and doing well, and we'll call once he's out of recovery.

When the doctor comes in, and he starts talking about exactly what they did, I zone out. I can't handle the talk of everything they did to his face. No wonder he's sore.

* * *

This becomes a routine for us. Every two weeks, he's in another surgery, and the waiting for him doesn't get any easier. Thankfully, Mom, Dad, Becky, and Johnny join me for each

141

one.

Now, I talk almost daily to his parents, keeping them informed of what's going on.

I'm sitting next to him, waiting for him to wake up from yet another surgery, which thankfully, is the last one.

He wakes up with a groan, and I'm there with water for him. His eyes open and focus on me. It's been a habit after each surgery for us to have a moment, when his blue eyes are focused on me for the first time, and that look does something to me.

It's like our souls are reconnecting after being apart. When the spell is broken, I smile.

"So, I have a surprise for you," I tell him.

"What's that, angel?"

I hold up a phone, and he looks confused.

"What? Is it on your phone?"

"No, this is your phone."

"Nope, I shut my phone off, and it doesn't look like that."

I laugh. "Actually, I added you to my plan. I have a few long work days coming to get caught up, and I thought this way we can video chat, even after visiting hours. Maybe, I can give you a tour of the house."

"Angel." He says, his voice still rough and scratchy. "This is amazing, and I love it, but I'll pay for my own line."

"No, you will not, Noah. You just worry about getting better. Do you hear me? Once you're up and walking, and they release you, then you can argue about it. Until then, you let me do this for you." I tell him in my no nonsense voice.

"Deal. Now, get over here and cuddle with me." He says, holding out his arm.

The nurses here in recovery just smile, they know us well

142

by now. I crawl into bed with him, and the exhaustion from the last several weeks takes over.

# Chapter 25

## Noah

I get my bandages off tomorrow. Today, my physical therapist is meeting with me to see what progress I've made, so he can set up a plan because I'm starting PT soon. I've never been so happy and so willing to get my ass kicked every day.

When Parks comes in, I'm sitting with Lexi on the couch. He's my physical therapist and insists on being on a first name basis with me.

"Noah!" He says, walking into the room with a huge smile on his face.

After a small bit of chitchat, he pats me on the back. "Let's see what you can do!"

Helping me stand up, he puts me through some basic moves. I can stand on my good leg, but I'm a bit unsteady, using my right leg.

"You're making good progress, even if you don't see it. I'll have a fast paced program ready, so be prepared for the pain, because it won't be easy or fun." Parks says.

"I'm more than ready for it," I assure him.

As he leaves, I sit back on the couch and pull Lexi into my

side.

"I want you to promise you won't push yourself too far. You can do damage and set yourself back if you overdo it." Lexi says.

"I promise to do as Parks says," I tell her.

We don't get to continue the discussion, because Dr. Taylor walks in.

"Well, Noah how do you feel about removing those bandages?" He says.

"I thought that was tomorrow."

"Yes, but your nurse says everything is looking good, and you healed faster than expected, so we can do it today." Nerves hit me like I just ran into a wall. He and Lexi help me back to the bed, as Brooke prepares to help the doctor remove the bandages. Lexi is at my side, holding my hand, as they start.

"Now remember, there will be some swelling for a few weeks, but it will go away. You need to be careful that nothing is thrown at your face, no hitting your face and try not to sleep on this side. All that we went over before surgery." He reminds me.

He steps back.

"Noah..." Lexi gasps.

I clamp my eyes shut afraid of what I'll see on her face.

"How bad is it?" I ask her.

"Oh, Noah. You've always been sexy to me, but holy shit, you're hot."

My eyes snap open, and her face says it all. She's running her eyes over me, and there's a smile on her face.

"I remember seeing you before when I'd be there with my brother, and I always thought you were good looking, Noah. I wasn't the only one. How you settled for Whitney I will never

145

know. But Noah, you know, it's different, but it's sexy as fuck."

Hearing her cuss like that for the first time gives me the courage to pick up the mirror Brooke placed in my lap and take a look at my new face.

There's some swelling, and it's evident around my eye mostly. There's a scar down the center of my forehead, the skin is a little rough near my ear, and the corner of my mouth. But where the skin was jagged and raised before, it's smooth now. If you look closely, you can see the different skin grafts, because each is a slightly different color.

Almost like Dr. Taylor notices that's what I'm looking at he speaks.

"The color will even out over the next four to six weeks, as the grafts heal. You won't be able to tell them apart."

I just shake my head, "It looks so much better than I thought possible."

"Can I touch him?" Lexi asks.

"Yes, just very gently. If it starts to hurt Noah, you speak up." The doctor says. He then gives me some care instructions, and the doctor and Brooke leave the room.

Lexi hasn't taken her eyes off of me, and when my eyes lock with her, the rest of the world falls away. I realize then it doesn't matter what anyone else thinks of me, only what this amazing woman in front of me thinks.

She leans forward and gently runs a finger down the scar on my forehead. I close my eyes, don't move, and just feel. Her fingers sweep over my eyebrow and next to my eye, over my cheek, and down to my mouth, where scars meet my lips, before replacing her finger with her lips.

At first, she kisses me gently, like she's afraid to hurt me. I wrap my hand behind her neck and pull her in, deepening the kiss, bringing her closer to me. She comes willingly and climbs into my lap, turning to straddle me. As her body sinks against mine, we never break the kiss.

It's a passionate kiss but still somehow gentle, and she doesn't try to push it further.

When we break apart, I rest my forehead against hers, and we are both breathing hard and holding on to each other. This moment is one I wish I could stay in forever. I have my girl in my arms, and everything is good.

Tomorrow, brings change, as neither of us knows what PT will hold, so tomorrow we start a new normal.

# Chapter 26

## Lexi

We have been in a good routine for about a week now. Noah goes to PT and comes back sore, but with a smile on his face. Brooke comes in and assesses his pain, he eats lunch, and then we nap. Waking up, he does some moves Parks gave him for his sore muscles, and then we spend the rest of the evening together until visiting hours are over.

Dr. Taylor has been in a few times to check on Noah, and he's here again today.

"You're looking really good." Dr. Taylor says, after checking out Noah.

"We'll be moving you to the rehab part of the hospital probably tomorrow since you don't need to be here anymore."

That catches my attention, so I follow him out into the hallway.

"What do you mean he doesn't need to be here anymore?" I ask him.

"Well, he only needs his PT and any appointments with his therapists. Many patients can do that from home. However, because Noah doesn't have a place to go, we move him to the rehab wing and help transition him out." Dr. Taylor says.

"So, if he has someplace to go, he can go home?"

"Yes, but he told me he doesn't have any place to go."

I rub my forehead. What is Noah thinking?

"When I was stationed back at Fort Hood, they had a military rehab home, where we could send guys," Dr. Taylor explains. "All their appointments were handled on the grounds, and they had their own rooms and all sorts of activities to attend. Plus, they had men in the same position to bond with."

"There's no place like that here?" I ask him.

"Sadly, no."

"Is the place in Fort Hood run by the military?"

"No, it was run by a couple. They had the military seal of approval and military funding, but it was privately owned."

"Do you have any information on it?"

He pulls out a pen and starts writing on his clipboard. "Their names are Judy and Keith, and this is their website." He says, handing me a piece of paper.

"So, if Noah had a place to stay, he could be released?"

"Yes." He nods.

"What does he need? Anything special?" I ask.

"Someone to get him to and from appointments, because he won't be cleared to drive for a while. He'll need someone to make sure he takes his medicine and be there in case he needs help. He's still unsteady, so no stairs or walking long distances, until cleared by PT. He also shouldn't be left alone for long periods of time, until his therapist clears him."

"Then, he can stay with me. I have an eight bedroom home. The master bedroom is on the main floor with an attached bathroom, and I have plenty of extra rooms to set up anything he needs."

Dr. Taylor looks surprised. "Well, if Noah is okay with it, I don't see why not."

He hands me a pack of paperwork on caring for him at home. I flip through it.

"Give me a week to get it set up. I need to redo the room, so it's easier for him to get around. I've been using the area for my work."

"Sounds good. We will move him to the rehab wing, until then."

I flip through the pack of papers, glancing over recommended items to have on hand, before stomping back into Noah's room and closing the door. I stand at the foot of the bed and cross my arms, glaring at him.

"Uh oh," he says and sits up straighter on the bed.

"You told the doctor you have no place to go?"

"I don't." He shrugs.

"Yeah, you do. You will stay with me. The doctor gave me this packet of information, and I'll get the house ready."

"Lexi…"

"No, Noah. This isn't negotiable. You don't deserve to be cramped in the hospital any longer than you have to be, and as of today, you don't have, too. The master bedroom is on the main floor, so you'll have a bathroom, and there are several rooms near, but we can make it into anything you need or want. Since I can work anywhere, I'll take you to and from appointments. Don't fight me on this, Noah." I say and finally take a deep breath.

"Come here, angel." He says with a smile on his face.

I walk over to the side of his bed, and he pulls me down for a kiss.

"No fighting." He agrees and looks into my eyes. "You're

amazing Lexi, and I feel like I don't deserve you."

"Noah, it's me who doesn't deserve you. Now, if you'll excuse me, I need to go shopping." I wave the packet of the paper Dr. Taylor gave me. "I will see you tomorrow."

I kiss him on the cheek and head home. When I walk in the front door, I stop to take a look around. This big, old house is going to have to work for Noah. If we come in through the side door, he can easily get to the master bedroom. The bathroom has a walk-in shower, so that isn't an issue. My office is in the room across the hall from the master, so I can work nearby.

The kitchen is a little further away, but I can move the table I have in the kitchen nook to the room next to my office, and there's another smaller room that can be set up, as a small gym for him. It can be Noah's wing until he's able to move around the house more easily. That way he can get to the back porch for some outside time, too.

As I walk to the other side of the house where the kitchen, living room, and formal dining room are, I begin to see the house with new eyes. I always knew this house would reveal what its purpose would be, and I think it's yelling at me right now.

I head into my office and pull up the rehab home in Texas that the doctor told me about. It looks like a bed-and-breakfast with a few differences. It seems to be smaller than my house, but the grounds have the same acreage. I shoot them an email with a few questions, before pulling up an online store to order something for Noah. Though, I go a bit overboard, there's plenty of room, and I want him to feel like this is his home, too.

The rooms need to be painted and touched up, so I call Becky to tell her my plans, and she calls a few other wives, and their guys are ready to help. We make plans to meet tomorrow to get going on my idea.

Then, I go to the store and get the paint we'll need, plus cleaning supplies, and a few other things.

When I get home, I have an email reply from the rehab home in Texas. The owner invited me out to the place, so I call Becky.

"I'll be heading out for town for a few days. It's work related, so can you and Johnny hang out with Noah?"

"Of course, but I know you, this isn't work."

"It's kind of is, but I promise to explain everything when I get home."

"I'll hold you to that."

My next call is to my mom and dad. I ask them to supervise the work being done on the house, while I'm away. They both jump at the chance, and I think my dad is happy to have something to do.

So, I email the rehab home back and get everything set up for a visit. The owner insists I stay with them, so it makes travel plans easy.

I go to bed with a smile on my face. Things are starting to fall into place, and I know longer feel like my life is on hold, as I try to figure out my next steps. I'm taking my next steps, and I can't wait to see where they lead.

# Chapter 27

**Noah**

When Lexi walks into the room today, she has a huge smile on her face, and it's contagious.

"Hey, angel," I say and kiss her, as she sits on the couch next to me.

"Well, the house plans are in motion, and so many people are willing to help out, that it should be done sooner than I expected. Johnny and Becky will be in to see you tomorrow because I have to go on a work trip for a few days. But we can talk on the phone every night."

I hate the idea of being away from her, but I don't want to stop her from doing what she needs to or wants to either.

"So, tell me more about these house plans," I say.

"Well, there are two empty rooms near the master. One will be set up like a home gym with stuff your doctor recommended, and the other as whatever you want. For now, I have it as a makeshift living room dining area, so you don't have to go to the other side of the house. I even ordered you a folding wheelchair to explore the house, even though I know you hate using it."

"I do, but I'll use it to be near you."

"Well, I have to head out and get packed for my trip. It was kind of last minute."

"Be safe, angel."

"Always." She smiles and leans in to kiss me.

I need more of her, so I pull her into my lap and deepen the kiss.

"Going to miss you."

"Me too, and I promise to hurry back." She says, and with one more kiss, gets up and leaves.

I watch her go, and as soon as she's gone, the nerves hit me again. Moving in with her is a big step, and it could change everything. The thought of not having to say goodbye and being able to hold her in my arms every night is exciting, but I don't want her to get tired of taking care of me. Right then, I vow to do everything I can to get better faster for her.

Officially bored, I get in my wheelchair and go to the rehab wing to see Easton. I stop in the doorway and knock.

He turns to look at me but says nothing, just nods his head.

"Got myself a new mug. It's still weird to look in the mirror, but Lexi likes it, and since she has to look at me every day, I guess that's all that matters." I tell him.

He turns and studies my face. "They did a good job."

"Yeah, hurt like a son of a bitch, though. I just kept thinking I have to be crazy to choose this kind of pain after everything."

Easton just nods.

"Lexi is going to be gone for a few days for work. Is it okay if I came to visit more, while she's gone?"

Again, he just nods his head. So, I launch into the story of how last time Lexi was gone her brother had me watching those pawn shop shows one after another, and how they had to be staged, and why I wondered was there that much interest in pawn shops.

When they bring dinner, I head back to my room. I need to talk to Lexi about coming back to visit with Easton. I don't like the idea of him sitting here and having no visitors after I leave. I'm sure she won't mind.

It will be easier to visit him tomorrow, anyway, once they move my room. I start making some plans for my time away from Lexi. The more I have to do, the less I can worry.

\* \* \*

## Lexi

I'm so lost in thought leaving the hospital that I almost trip over the cutest dog. I look up and find a girl about my age, trying to pull the dog out of the way.

"I'm sorry. I was preoccupied." I apologize.

"It's okay. Molly here doesn't always pay attention either." She says.

"I didn't know they allowed dogs in the hospital."

"Well, she's a therapy dog, and I come in when I can. I try for once a week, and let the guys spend some time with her, it seems to help. I'm Paisley by the way." She holds out her hand.

I shake it, "Lexi."

"You should ask to see Noah Carr. He's my boyfriend. He'll be coming home soon, but I have to go out of town for a few days, so he could use the company."

155

"I'll ask about him for sure."

"Can I pet her?" I ask, pointing to the dog.

"Yep, she's off duty now!" Paisley says.

I lean down and pet Molly, a golden retriever, who eats it right up. "Aren't you an attention hound?" I say while petting her. Then, my to-do list flashes into my mind, so I stand up and offer Paisley a smile. "Well, I hope I'll see you around."

When I get home, my mom and dad are there, and we go over the plans for the rooms over dinner, while I pack.

"I'm so proud of you for doing this, letting someone back in." My dad says.

I can tell he's excited to have something to do. Mom has been keeping a tight leash on him, since his surgery.

The next day Becky takes me to the airport, and I'm off to Texas. The owners Judy and Keith meet me at the gate and drive me to their home, which is on the property.

"So, do you want to get settled in or take a tour of the place?" Keith asks.

"Tour, please!" I say, and Judy laughs.

"I thought you'd say that."

We use a golf cart to get from their house to the main building.

"This ranch house was in my family for a few generations, along with the land. I had no interest in farming it, but after I came back injured from my military time, we had this idea and kind of ran with it." Keith says.

"We added on to the house. It's now fifteen rooms. There's a common room, family meeting area, and a game room all right off the lobby." Judy says as we enter.

"This looks almost like a resort," I say.

"We wanted it to have that atmosphere. These men spend

156

so much time in the hospital that we didn't want them to feel like they were still there." She says.

"I like that idea. That way, I'd be able to keep a lot of the history of the home." I say, thinking out loud.

"Upstairs is all rooms, and we have several rooms on the main level over there," Keith says, pointing to the hallway on the right.

"Down here is the dining room, physical therapy room, an office for the doctor to meet with patients, and our offices," Judy says, taking me down the hall to the left and showing me each room.

We step out onto the back porch.

"Over there is our barn. We have equine therapy. It's great for the guys who like to work in the barn, taking care of the horses just as much as riding them. They can ride without doing the therapy, but the therapy does get them up on a horse to ride. We have an indoor pool area there." Keith points to a large building that looks almost like a warehouse.

"It's good for helping gain muscle strength back, and some guys use it, as stress relief, too," Judy adds.

We head back into their office and go over all the details of getting set up, the paperwork I'd need, how to set up a nonprofit, and getting military approval. It all makes my head spin, and when they hand me stacks and stacks of paperwork to take home, I'm even more overwhelmed.

"So, tell me about this place you want to use," Judy says.

"It's an old plantation home. I figure once fully renovated I can get twenty-one rooms, plus a library, a large lobby area for families, a dining room, offices, and a PT room. There's a barn on the property that needs to be restored. I have an area set aside for a garden, and I've read that can help in rehabilitation as well. Down the road, I'd like to build an aquatic center. There are fifty acres, so plenty of room."

"Will you live on the property?" Keith asks.

"Yes. There's a couple living down the road, and they're getting ready to sell. They have thirty acres that used to belong to the plantation back in the day. I figure I can move there and give the land back to Oakside, and then have more room to add on later."

Once I get back to my room, I collapse on my bed. What a wealth of knowledge those two have, and they are willing to share it all. I have so much to do when I get home.

I knew the house would show me what its purpose would be, and I know this is it.

Before I pass out, I call Noah, because as busy as I was, I still miss him like crazy.

I decide not to tell him right away what I'm doing, at least, not until I bring him home and can show him. And I can't wait!

# Chapter 28

**Lexi**

When I leave the airport, I decide to grab my keys and head right into see Noah. I get to the hospital with only ten minutes of visiting hours left, but I sneak into his new room. I intend to stay until they kick me out.

"Nice digs," I enter, closing the door behind me.

This room is a bit nicer with a little less of a hospital feel to it, but there's no mistaking you're still in a hospital.

"Hey, angel. Did you just get in?" He asks and pats the spot next to him on the couch.

"Yes, and I came straight here. I wanted to see you," I snuggle next to him and rest my head on his shoulder.

"Tell me about your trip."

"Not just yet, it's part of your surprise."

"You went to Texas as a surprise for me?" He says his voice laced with confusion.

"Partly. Just trust me, you'll see."

"The house should be ready any day now, so don't get too comfortable in this room." I joke.

"I won't," he chuckles.

"There's just one more thing for you to decide," I say, slightly nervous to bring it up.

"What's that?" He pulls me closer like he can sense my nerves. This is Noah, so he probably can.

"You need to decide if you want to share a room with me, or if you want your own space," I say.

Noah wastes no time in pulling me into his lap, and I turn to straddle him, so I can see his face and keep my weight on my legs and off of him, as much as possible. I wrap my arms around his neck and soak him in. He settles his hands on my waist like he plans to hold me in place.

"Do you really think I'd pass up the chance to sleep with you every night? To have you in my arms all night long? Angel, you keep the nightmares away and make me feel safe. There's no way I'd be able to sleep, knowing you're under the same roof, but not in my arms. The question is are you ready for that? Because it's not just me there to rehab. It means we're moving in together; taking this to the next level." He says his voice steady, but his eyes show how unsure he is.

I smile and kiss him softly. "I love you, Noah. So yes, I'm ready for this."

There's a sharp intake of breath from him, "I love you too, Angel, so damn much." He leans in and kisses me passionately.

The more we kiss, the harder I feel him getting between my legs. I don't want to break the spell, so I keep kissing until I'm so turned on, I need relief.

"Noah…" I whisper against his lips.

"I feel it too, angel." He tightens the grip on my hips and grinds me against his hard length, making me moan.

As he watches me, he does it again and then sets a steady rhythm of grinding that has me cumming so fast that I can barely catch my breath. I collapse against him, my head on his shoulder, as he rubs my back.

I finally sit up and look at him and smile. "Your turn," I reach for him.

He grabs my wrist, bringing it to his mouth, and places a kiss in the center of my hand.

"It's always about you, angel. Besides, I don't think I'm ready to know yet." He whispers the last part.

I nod and lean in to kiss him again.

"Then, I should get home. Mom and Dad are there waiting on me, and we have some plans to make." I wink at him, before heading out.

Once home, I'm greeted with life. Instead of the dark, quiet rooms that always await me, there's life in this house, and I have to say I like it. I find Mom and Dad in the room next to my office that will be a makeshift living room and dining area for Noah.

"Hey, baby." Mom hugs me when I walk into the room. "The guys got the gym set up next door, and we are just putting the final touches on this room."

Looking around, I see a TV and couch area in one corner, and on the other side, a small dining room table and chairs to seat four. There's also a recliner and a bookshelf. It all has my mom's decorating touch to it, and I can't wait to show Noah.

"It's so much better than the hospital room he's been staying in," I say. "Do you have a moment? I want to talk to you about something before you go."

"Of course." My dad says as they sit down on the couch, while I perch on the edge of the recliner facing them.

"Well, you know Noah is moving in here for his rehab, but we talked, and this is more than that. It's him *moving* in."

Mom smiles, "We figured as much, sweetheart."

"Okay well, I finally know what I want to do with this house. You know I went to Texas to meet with a couple, who run a rehabilitation center for wounded military men and women. They turned their ranch home into a facility, and they work with the military to cover the cost for care for the soldiers. It's a place that Johnny and Noah would be able to do PT and heal, once they were ready to leave the hospital. They provide counselors to help the soldiers transition back to the civilian world, get them jobs, places to live, all of it." I stop and take a deep breath when I realize I was rambling.

"I want to do that here." I watch my parents, as they turn to look at each other.

They don't say anything, so I keep talking.

"Judy and Keith, that's their names. One of the things they told me, is there's a ministry that helped them build on to the house and get it ready, and it was done for free, because of the cause. She got me their info, and I thought maybe since my dad owns a construction company, he would be willing to help. I know you normally flip houses, but I trust you to oversee the guys. They also suggested contacting a local college to see if any grant writers are willing to help out for the experience. We'll have to put our heads together to get some publicity and fundraisers going. They sent me home with so much paperwork it makes my head spin." I tell them.

"Lexi," Mom laughs. "We love the idea."

"Of course, I'll be here during construction; we want to help any way we can." Dad continues, "As long as you keep as much of the historical elements, as we're able." He says, looking around the room.

"That's the plan. I want it to feel like a bed-and-breakfast, not a hospital. On the rough plans I drew up, I was planning for twenty-one rooms." I go on to tell them about the plans for the place and about reaching out to buy the colonial house next door.

I have enough money left over from Tyler to buy the house and get renovations going, but we need to start on grants and fundraising sooner rather than later to get the place ready to take patients.

By the time they leave, it's almost midnight. But the time flew by, as we talked about plans, and they're genuinely excited and want to help any way they can. Besides, I think they're happy for me to have a purpose, and they'd support me even if I'd said that I want to turn it into a strip club.

"One more thing." I stop them before they leave. "I'm hoping to get Noah moved in this week, so maybe this weekend, you guys along with Becky and Johnny can come over, and we can do family dinner here?"

Both my parent's eyes water and I know why. I haven't hosted a family dinner, since Tyler died. They have eaten here sure, but normally, it was when they'd push their way in to make sure I was okay, but I never openly hosted dinner.

"We'll be here," Mom says, before hugging me.

I'm so pumped up I know I won't be able to sleep, so I spend some time getting the master bedroom ready, making sure he has half of the huge walk-in closet, and cleaning out one of the dressers for him to use. Then, I check that the second sink in the bathroom is ready for his stuff.

Am I really letting a guy into my life? Taking a breath, I wait for the panic to come, but it doesn't. I wander into the living room and stare at the photos of Tyler.

"Somehow, I get this was your plan all along," I say smiling.

163

# Chapter 29

**Noah**

Oh, man, did PT kick my butt today. But this is a good kind of aching, one that says I'm making progress, and one that says I'm healing. I will take this kind of sore any day.

On my way back to my room, I stop to see Easton and knock like always.

"Hey," I say, but he doesn't even look my way.

His nurse walks up beside me, "Today, is a bad day, so maybe, try again tomorrow?" I nod and take one last look at the tortured man on the other side of the room.

"I'm here if you ever need me. To talk, yell, or hit something. I'm here." I tell him.

Still no reaction, so I turn and head back to my room. I find Lexi there waiting on me, and my mood lifts instantly.

"Angel," I say, as she stands and leans in to kiss me. She helps me from the wheelchair to the couch and snuggles right up to me.

"Guess what." She says.

"What?"

"I talked to your doctor, and it looks like you get to come

home today!"

I'm floored. I was expecting to be here a few more days, and if I'm honest, the thought of leaving this place seemed more like a dream than something that was actually going to happen.

"Really?"

"Yep, my parents kicked butt getting everything done, while I was gone. Becky brought in a lot of help, too."

I'm freaking excited mostly, because I'm so done being in this hospital, but also because it means Lexi and I get to start the next part of our relationship. Yes, we are moving in, but it also means I can start courting her like she deserves. I'll hold her in my arms at night, and there are no more goodbyes.

I also can't wait to see this house she's so passionate about. To see this space with my own eyes, one that holds her heart, and she's allowing me to share. The best part is me being able to leave.

As we are waiting on all the discharge paperwork, she helps me pack up my stuff.

Finally, the doctor comes in to go over my limitations, no lifting over ten pounds, and I'm to stick to my diet, so no spicy foods.

Then, he gives us referrals and prescriptions for things like my sleeping medicine, if I need them and more. Along with a ton of instructions and follow up appointments, we're ready to leave. Before we go, Lexi adds every appointment to the calendar on her phone.

Lexi takes me out in the wheelchair, and Brooke is there to say goodbye.

"It's always hard when patients go home. We get so attached, and though, this is what we have been working for all this time, I'm still going to miss you." Brooke hugs Lexi.

"Since Noah is no longer your patient, why don't we do lunch next week? You're my friend, and I don't want to lose that. Plus, I want to pick your brain on a project I'm working on." Lexi says.

I perk right up because she hasn't mentioned a project to me, but maybe, it's part of what she wants to talk about when we get to the house, so I let it go.

"Of course, you have my number. Call me, and we'll set it up," Brooke says.

As we make our way outside, I notice the little things. The sun on my face, the slight breeze in my hair, and the noise of the hospital parking lot. Maybe, Easton is on to something, enjoying the outside.

Lexi helps me into her SUV, and once we're settled, she looks over at me.

"Everything okay, angel?"

"Yeah, just want to savor this. I have been waiting for the day that I can take you home. It's weird having someone else in the car, but I like it." She smiles.

I roll down the window and enjoy my freedom on the drive out of town. Reaching over, I take Lexi's hand, and this feels normal and right. After a little drive, we turn down an old country road, and I know we're getting close to her house. There are a few places out here, but not many, and there's still a lot of land.

"All this land used to belong to Oakside, but it was sold off over the years. This house here," she points to a colonial style home on her left. "Is up for sale. It has thirty acres and runs right alongside my property."

When she turns into the driveway, there's an old iron gate in front of it.

"The gate is original, but it's been updated and made electric." She rolls down her window and punches in a code.

We make our way down a long driveway with oak trees on both sides, forming a tree tunnel.

"You weren't kidding. This is beautiful," I say.

"It's my favorite part of the outside of the house," Lexi says with a huge smile, and her enthusiasm is catching, making me smile, too.

A minute later the house comes into view, and I'm pretty sure my jaw hits the ground. In front of us, is one of the most beautiful Greek Revival homes I've ever seen. It looks like one of the plantation homes you see in magazines or travel brochures. It's a large two-story home with what I'm assuming is an attic window, making a small third floor. There are six huge two-story columns along the front porch that runs the length of the front of the house.

The second floor has a balcony, and the windows and doors are exactly the same on the first floor.

"The front of the house is untouched as the day it was built, but there was a fire, so the back of the house has been reconstructed. The sides were added on later, but they match the rest of the house." Lexi says.

She's talking about the two-story L shaped wings on either side of the house. Just like she said, it looks just like a true southern plantation home.

Lexi pulls around to the left side of the house.

"This entrance is closer to the master bedroom, so you should be able to walk if you want."

"Let's use the wheelchair. I want to see the house."

Really, I'm still sore from PT, and I don't trust myself right now, but taking it into the house, is the perfect excuse, and

Lexi doesn't even question it.

We enter into a decent sized mudroom with lots of places to hang coats and store shoes and other items. Then, we enter a hallway that's filled with natural light. There are a lot of windows ahead on my left, looking out over a small courtyard.

"Well, you are officially the first patient of Oakside Military Rehabilitation Home," Lexi says, as she stops beside me.

"What?" I ask, thinking I missed something.

"I have too much to tell you, but first, a quick tour. This is your wing." Lexi moves with me down the hall where another short corridor is off to my left filled with windows on one side, looking over a courtyard.

"Down here is your home gym and living room dining area," Lexi points down the hallway to my left.

"The room over there is my office, and we added a desk, so you can use it as well," Lexi gestures to the door up ahead on the right.

"And this is your room." She opens the door on my right.

"Our room." I correct her. I have been waiting to share a bed with her, and I'm not letting her out of that so easily.

The room is larger than any room I've ever had in my life. The large king size bed actually looks small against the wall.

"This wasn't part of the original house, but they did good, including some of the same woodwork and all. In here, is the closet." Lexi opens a door on the left side of the room.

It's almost a small room in itself. There are shelves to hang clothes on either side. One is packed with clothes that look like Lexi's, and the other side has a few clothes I recognize.

"I unpacked some of your boxes that were labeled clothes. This side is yours. Now, over here is the bathroom." Lexi opens the door next to the closet, and inside, is a bathroom that is about the size of my room in the barracks. There are double sinks, a large walk-in shower, and a claw foot tub.

"This place is beautiful," I say, taking in all the little details. "Now, what was that about Oakside Military Rehabilitation Home?"

# Chapter 30

**Noah**

She takes me into her office, and I can see Lexi in here. The curtains are open, and there's a ton of natural light. A desk against one wall that is messy, but I know makes sense to her. Her computer, several bookcases that hold some books, and photo props. On the wall are photos, and everything looks like it's been moved to make room for the now empty desk she said would be for me to use.

Lexi grabs a folder from her desk and brings it over and hands it to me. Instead of taking the folder, I pull her down onto my lap and wrap my arms around her waist, pulling her close.

"So, I went to Texas to visit a military rehabilitation home there. It's a place where you could be now, while you finish PT, where Johnny could have been, and where Easton could be." She says.

"There isn't anything like that here?" I ask, thinking the idea would be more popular, and they'd have places like this all over.

"No, but this is what I want to do. I'd like to turn it into

170

Oakside Military Rehabilitation Home. That's why I was in Texas. The couple who runs the one out there invited me and showed me around. It's like a bed-and-breakfast with activities, and the guys have more freedom than a hospital, and I think it's a better place to heal. There's a PT room, and a doctor comes to the home for the appointments. What do you think?"

This idea is amazing. Giving guys like me a place to be, a little independence outside the hospital. It might be just what Easton needs. I can't forget about him or leave him behind, but I'm not sure how to reach him either. For now, I'll shelf that for another day.

"Angel, I love the idea."

"Yeah?"

"Yep, I've been trying to figure out what to go to school for, but now I know," I tell her.

"What?"

"Business management, so I can help you run this place."

As the thought takes root, so many ideas start churning in my head. I love this idea, and being able to be a part of it, would be amazing.

"You want to help me run it?" Her eyes light up. "I love that idea, Noah. You'd be such a help to the guys because you've been in their shoes."

I nod, "Sometimes, you just need to feel like you aren't alone. The guys here could help each other. Have you thought about renovations?"

"Yes, so this won't be the first floor bedrooms. There's room behind the staircase where we can put in an elevator, and then the living room and dining room would make a good lobby. In the other wing, we would have the dining room, library with computers, and the PT room." She pulls out her phone and shows me photos of the place in Texas.

"The basement would have a few bedrooms on the back since it's a walkout basement. My office, I mean our office, would be there, along with room for the staff, the kitchen, laundry, doctor's office, and storage."

I really like that she corrected herself, our office. The idea of working with her is getting me excited for this project, and the more I think about it, the more I love it.

"With a little work, we can get ten bedrooms on the second floor and two more on the third floor. I'd like each room to have its own bathroom, but we'll have to talk to my dad about how to make it work." She says.

"I know you haven't seen it, but there's a beautiful fireplace in the living room I'd like to feature in the lobby. I want to make that a room where guests can relax, and so can their visitors. Picture a large living room. All in all, we would have twenty-one rooms. I'd like to keep the porches and courtyard for the guys to use and make sure they have enough benches and rocking chairs. I want to put in a garden. My plans include a section with flowers and a section with fruit and vegetables to use in the kitchen. Did you know there's a type of therapy used in gardens to help those with anxiety? The barn can be fixed up and used for equine therapy as well."

"I think you forgot one thing," I tell her.

"What's that?" She asks, pursing her lips trying to think.

"Where will we live, angel?"

"Well, assuming you don't tire of me." She sighs.

"Lexi, never," I tell her. "You're it for me. I feel it in my bones. I plan to make you my wife someday, soon if I have my way."

Her eyes go wide, and she opens her mouth to speak, but

closes it again before she keeps on with what she was saying. I want her to know I'm serious, and where I stand.

"Remember the colonial I pointed out on the way here?" She says.

"The one that's for sale?"

"Yep, I talked to the owner, and they love the idea of Oakside, and the land going back to help the soldiers so much, that they're willing to sell it, and at a really good price. It has five bedrooms, and the basement is set as its own apartment with two more rooms in case we need it. I was thinking we keep one acre for the house, and the other twenty-nine go back to Oakside. I have enough money left over from Tyler's insurance to buy it and start on some small renovations. Though, we'll need grants and fundraisers for the rest." She says.

"I love the idea." I can tell there's more she wants to tell me from the look on her face, so I squeeze her hip. "What else?"

"Well, there's a place just beyond the barns. It's some old building damaged in a fire but never rebuilt. I think it would be a perfect place to build some guest cottages for families to stay in. Then, I'd like to build an aquatics center with a pool, sauna, and hot tubs, too. It's all in the future, but our main focus would be getting this place set up. While we work on the second and third floors, I think we can get everything going on the first floor and ready for patients."

She looks over at her desk. "Oh, I contacted the local college to find some grant writers to volunteer their time to help get us some money. Judy and Keith pointed me towards a ministry that will help with renovations, and my dad agreed to supervise them and help out, too."

This house was always Lexi's dream. So much so, that Tyler made sure if anything were to happen to him, that she'd still get her dream. So, I have to know.

"This house was your dream, Lexi. Are you sure this is what you want? Are you okay not living here?"

She laughs. That was not the reaction I was expecting.

"I'll be spending most of my days here. I want to be as hands on as possible. And knowing we will be helping so many people, guys like you and Johnny? I can't imagine a better way to fill up this home."

"I agree," trying to hide a yawn that takes over.

As excited as I am about all this, between PT and the excitement of getting out of the hospital, I'm worn out. Lexi doesn't miss it, though.

"Come on, let's get you settled in for a nap. I have a few phone calls to make, and then I'll join you."

I follow her in the master bedroom, our bedroom.

"Which side do you normally sleep on?" I ask.

"Well, normally the right side closest to the door, but I think you should take it because it will be easier for you. I can move my stuff to the other side."

"No, I can sleep over there. It's not a big deal," I tell her.

She leans over, putting her hands on the armrest of my wheelchair, and stops me from moving. She looks right into my eyes, and I know she means business.

"Noah, you're taking this side, because it's easier for you. When you're up and moving again, we can talk, but either you take this side, or I will go sleep upstairs." She raises an eyebrow in a challenge.

"Fine, but as soon as I'm moving better, we are switching sides."

"If you think so," she smirks, as I get into bed.

# Chapter 31

**Lexi**

When I make my way back to my room, after talking with people applying for the grant writing position, I find Noah asleep. It's weird having someone in my bed again, but I like that I have someone to climb into bed with.

I just watch him sleep. He seems to sleep better here than he did in the hospital, and I like to think it's because he feels safe here. Making my way to the other side, I try not to wake him climbing in, but the moment the bed dips, he turns to face me.

"Everything okay?" He mumbles, still half asleep.

"Yes, I have a few interviews lined up for the grant writer position. They'll do it at no cost to us to gain experience and the same for the charity coordinators. I get to start all that paperwork tomorrow. Now, go back to sleep." I tell him.

"I drifted a bit, but I wanted to hear what you were up, too." He pulls me to lie on his shoulder. My body is pressed as close to his as he can get it. It's comfortable, and the fact that I'm on his left side doesn't escape me. I'm careful of him, but I love that he's confident enough to not hide his scars from me.

"Well, tomorrow I'll work on all the military paperwork. Oh, and my dad is sending some guys over to get measurements, so they can get a blueprint made and see if my ideas will work," I say, snuggling into him, as close as I can get.

The next thing I know, I jolt awake. I'm in my bed, but in someone's arms, and I jump out of bed before I realize it's Noah.

"Lexi, what's wrong?" He sits up and looks around the room.

I run my hands over my face, "Nothing, I guess this will take some more getting used to than I realized." I groan, climbing back into bed.

Noah chuckles and lays back down. "It was weird waking up here too, but I smelled you, and it didn't matter where I was, I had you in my arms. I'm going to love waking up like this."

"I've gotten so used to being alone, especially here, and this has been my sanctuary, so I just need time," I say.

"We have all the time in the world."

I yawn and stretch, as his eyes run hungrily down my body before he leans in and kisses me. The kiss is over too quickly, but I know I need to feed us, so I don't take it further.

"What would you like for dinner? BLT sandwiches or spaghetti?"

"Spaghetti sounds good. Let me get up. I want to watch you cook." He says.

It's fun to actually have someone in the kitchen with me again. Having Noah here is showing me little things, I didn't realize I was missing.

Once dinner is going, my phone rings.

"Sorry," I say to Noah, and he just smiles.

* * *

## Noah

While Lexi is on the phone, I look out of the window over the backyard. There's a lot of open space out there, and in my mind's eye, I can see patients out there on the back porch, enjoying the sun before dinner.

Maybe, working out on the lawn. Summer activities for the patients, BBQs, and water activities. I can see it all, everything Lexi has been talking about, and I want it more than I could ever imagine.

Her dream is infectious and has easily overtaken me. During my time in the hospital, I kept trying to figure out my next step. What I could do with my life. The skills the military gave me didn't translate outside in the civilian world, and most companies wouldn't want me to be the face their customers see. Then, in one moment, Lexi gave me a path, a purpose.

She gave me something I didn't even know I wanted, and now, I can't imagine my life without this opportunity. It's a clear path to attending college, getting my business degree, and helping her run it.

Lexi gets off the phone and lets out a little sequel.

"Good news?" I ask, pulled from my new daydream.

"The college put out my request for interns for the charity organizer, and I already got a call! The girl is really sweet and is super excited to help out. She'll be here tomorrow for an interview. I told her once we open there's an option to go full time if we work well together. His brother is Army, so she loves the idea. I want to have people around that are as passionate as I am, as we are." She says, coming over to give me a hug.

Her enthusiasm for all this is contagious, and I smile big. As I wrap my arms around her waist, I want to keep her smile there always, and I want many more years with her, as happy as she is right now.

"So, do we have plans for dinner tomorrow?" I ask her.

"No, why?"

"Well, I'd like to take you out on a date, a real date. We've done things completely backwards with me moving in before I have a chance to court you, or spoil you like you should be spoiled," I tell her.

"Well, I have been craving sandwiches from this deli near my parents' house..." She smiles, as she walks over.

I pull her into my lap, "Done." I say, right before I kiss her.

# Chapter 32

**Lexi**

As I'm getting ready for my date with Noah in an upstairs bedroom, I can't wipe the smile off my face. It's been such a long time since I got dressed up for a date. I try to keep my nerves at bay by thinking about today.

Earlier, Noah had his PT appointment with his new therapist, and he's willing to push Noah just like he wants. He gave us some great exercises to do at home and was impressed with our home gym.

Also, we had the interview with the charity coordinator intern. Her name is Mandy, and we got along great. She loves the idea of Oakside and even had some great ideas for fundraising. I gave her the position on the spot, and if she turns out to be as good as her interview, then I hope I can bring her on full-time.

Mandy was excited she could do a lot of the work from home but asked to be here, to see the transformation. She thinks we should document it in social media to build up hype and is taking the lead on that.

She left about an hour ago, so I came up here to get ready

and made Noah leave. He encouraged me to make this as much like a date as possible, and that means picking me up and everything. I'm finishing my makeup when the doorbell goes off. It takes me a minute to realize what it is because anyone who visits just comes in the side door, and I rarely get visitors who ring the doorbell.

Opening the front door, I find Noah, standing there with flowers and everything.

"You look stunning, angel." He says, as his eyes track down my body and back up again.

"You look pretty sexy there yourself," I tell him.

This is the first time I've seen Noah in jeans, and they look amazing on him. He's wearing a long sleeve shirt that hugs his muscles in all the right places.

His brown hair is a bit longer than it was when he was in the military, and it has an unruly curl around his ears.

"You ready to go?"

"Yep."

I take his arm, closing the door behind me. He walks me to the car, and even opens my door, even though I'm driving.

On the way there, we talk about his family, because I've been wanting to learn more about his sisters and him growing up.

When we arrive, I have one more question I have to ask. Placing my hand on his arm I look over at him. "You sure you're okay without your wheelchair?"

"I am. I'm feeling really good."

"You let me know, if you aren't, okay?"

"Promise. Now, wait there." He points his gaze at me, before getting out of the car.

I wait for him to come open my door, and I have to admit I really like this gentlemanly side of Noah. He wraps his arm around my waist and pulls me into his side, as we walk into the deli. When we get in line, I notice a boy looking at Noah's scars.

"Mom, that man has a huge scar on his face." The boy says a little louder than I think he meant, too.

Beside me, Noah goes stiff. This boy can't be more than ten, so I place my hand on Noah's arm, and then I turn to the boy and tap him on his shoulder. When he turns to look at me, his eyes go wide, like he didn't realize we heard him.

"You noticed his scar?" I ask him.

The boy just nods.

"Well, this is Noah. He was in the Marines and got that scar, fighting the bad guys who tried to attack him. He also saved my brother from the bad guys." I say, keeping things as simple as possible.

The boy's eyes are still wide, but they shoot over to Noah.

"He did?" He asks in wonder.

"Yep. He's pretty badass if you ask me." I say with a smile on my face.

"Wow." The boy says, and I feel Noah relax next to me.

The boy's mother leans down and whispers in his ear, and then the boy steps up to Noah and holds out his hand.

"Thank you for your service."

Noah shakes his hand, but it gains the attention of a few others in the lobby, who also thank Noah. We get our food and sit down, and Noah just stares at me.

"Thank you for that."

"No need to thank me, Noah. We're a team, and I've got you back, always."

He takes my hand in his and rubs his fingers over my knuckles.

"That means everything to me, angel."

We talk about the plans for Oakside, the next steps, and bringing in Mandy. How Johnny and Becky want to help out.

"I really want to bring Easton in as one of our first. I think he needs out of that hospital, and people to push him outside that room." Noah says.

"I agree. I want to help him, and I also want to see if we can convince Brooke to come with us. Then, there's this girl who does volunteer work, Paisley, who brings in therapy dogs. Maybe, we could add her to the team."

"Yes, she stopped by and said you sent her. I like that idea, and she was really nice. Where are you with the paperwork?"

"Well, I plan to finish up with the charity paperwork and submit it tonight. Then, it's the military paperwork next. Both the VA and the military have to sign off on the plans and everything before we can begin construction."

When we get home, Noah stops me outside the door.

"You okay?" I ask.

"I'm perfect. This is one of the best dates I can ever remember being on."

"It was pretty good, wasn't it?"

Ever so slowly, Noah leans in and kisses me so softly.

"Wouldn't be a date without a goodnight kiss," he whispers against my lips, before pulling away.

He follows me into my office and looks at the website of the rehab home in Texas, while I finish up the charity paperwork before we go to bed.

Before climbing into bed, I realize we're both in sweatpants and t-shirts and laugh.

"I think we can both consider wearing fewer clothes to bed," I say, changing into cotton shorts and a tank top, but when I come back out, Noah hasn't changed.

"What's wrong?" I ask.

He hesitates just a moment, and it hits me.

"You want to keep the scars covered," I say, and he nods and looks down at his feet.

I move to stand in front of him and take both his hands in mine.

"You know I find your scars sexy as hell, right?"

Again, he nods but doesn't say anything.

"Please, don't hide them from me, not here in our house. Out there with everyone else, I get it, but don't hide with me." I almost beg.

With a shaking breath, he takes off his shirt, and we climb into bed. He pulls the covers up over his chest, as I slowly pull the covers back. I watch his face, as I lightly trace the scars on this chest and down his arm.

He stares up at the ceiling, but he doesn't stop me. I trace the scars down his side to the waist of his pants, and there's no hiding that he's getting hard. I trail my hand down further and rub his cock over his pants.

"Lexi," he whispers.

"Want me to stop?"

"No."

I straddle his hips and lean down to kiss him, before trailing kisses down his neck on the scarred side of his body. I kiss the scars on his shoulder and down his chest, taking my time with each line and dip.

When my lips reach the waist of his pants, I move his pants down, kissing the scars on his leg. But when I go to remove his pants, he's not wearing underwear. His eyes are on me and hungry for more.

"Take your shirt off for me, angel." I do as he asks, and my shirt lands on the floor with his pants. I kiss all the scars on his other leg until I reach his rock, hard cock. Then, I take it and stroke him, and it's erotic, watching him watching me. When I lean in and take him in my mouth, he throws his head back on the pillow and grabs the sheets on the bed beside him.

I take him as far back in my mouth as I can, before sliding back up, and I continue to slowly work him. Each glide down his shaft, has him moaning my name louder and louder. As I taste him, I bring my hand up and cup his balls, before giving them a light tug, which makes his hips jerk.

He reaches out to grab hold of my hair, "Lexi, baby. Oh, God that feels so good... so good, angel," he says almost breathless.

The more I increase my efforts, the more his breathing quickens, and I feed off it. It's such a turn on seeing what I can do to this stunning man and have this kind of control over him. My clit throbs and my underwear are soaked, but I ignore it all and focus on him.

"So close..." He grits out just before I take him in as far as I can, feeling his cum coat the back of my throat. He shouts my name, as he cums.

Once he relaxes, I kiss his chest all the way up, enjoying the tremors I caused. When I lean in to kiss his mouth, he cradles the back of my head and flips me over, so I'm on my back, and he's on top of me.

The kiss is unlike any we have shared, it's more desperate. When I feel wetness on my cheeks, it takes me a minute to realize they are his tears. He rests his head in my neck, and I rub his back.

"You, okay?" I ask when he doesn't speak or move.

He nods, "I was scared that would never happen. That we

would never be able to…" He trails off and takes a deep breath, before leaning up and kissing me again.

His hand moves down my shoulder to my breasts, playing lightly with the nipple, before continuing down my side. He cups my pussy over my shorts, before pushing them to the side. When he runs a finger over my slit, he groans.

"Damn, baby, you're soaked. Did sucking my cock turn you on?" I gasp, because dirty talking Noah is something I didn't expect, and it excites me, so that I can't speak, and I just nod.

"You're perfect, angel. So damn perfect." He groans, before kissing me again at the same time he thrusts a finger into me, making me moan.

When he adds a second finger, my hips jerk, and he puts his weight on me enough to hold me in place. He turns his wrist slightly while stroking my clit with his thumb. Another small twist and he's hitting my g spot, and making me gasp. He's in so deep, and the feeling is intense.

He presses on that spot while taking one of my nipples into his mouth. He sucks hard causing me to cum so hard that I don't realize I'm screaming his name. When I'm finally able to open my eyes, I see him pull his fingers from my core and lick them clean.

"That was the sexiest thing I've ever seen, angel." Then, he reaches over and removes my shorts and panties.

He lies down and pulls me to him.

"I just want to sleep skin to skin." He murmurs into my neck.

So do I, more than I even realized.

# Chapter 33

**Noah**

I watch Lexi run around almost in a panic, putting away all her photography stuff and getting the dining room ready for dinner with her family.

"Angel, relax they're your family, and they have been here before." I try to calm her down.

"But I've never hosted family dinner here. I haven't hosted family dinner, since…" When she trails off, I know she means, since Tyler. Looking towards the fireplace where his photos are, it's almost like I'm being pulled to them, and before I know it, I'm standing in front of the fireplace, staring at them.

There's a photo of the two of them on their wedding day. Another on the beach with his arms around her, and her back to his chest. One of her standing next to him in uniform, and you can tell she had been crying.

"That was the last time I saw him." She says when she sees what photo I'm looking at.

"You should put up more photos around the house," I say, noticing she only has photos of him in here.

"It was easier this way. I didn't feel like he wasn't remembered, but if it was too hard, I could avoid this room."

"Your parents aren't expecting royalty to dinner, if anyone has something to be nervous about it's me," I tell her.

"Oh, they love you already, maybe more so than me." She jokes.

"Tell me what to do, and I'll do it, while you go get ready." With my marching orders in hand, I'm setting the table, when just as I finish, the doorbell rings.

"Oh, for God sakes. Who is it?" She rushes to the front door with me right behind her.

"Mom, Dad? Why are you at the front door, when you always come in the side door?"

"I reminded them that with you now living with a guy it might be best not to catch you unexpectedly." Johnny smiles.

"That's you and Becky! I have enough common sense to refrain, when I know I'm having guests coming over." She rolls her eyes and steps aside, as her parents, Moore, and his wife step in.

Both her parents greet me with a hug.

"Moore," I say and nod towards him.

"Christ, you saved my life and are living with my sister, so I think you can call me Johnny." He says, and then reaches out and shakes my hand.

His wife laughs and gives me a hug.

The girls head into the kitchen, and the guys follow me into the living room.

"How's your PT going?" Johnny asks.

"Really good. I'm able to walk a lot more now. There were only a few times I had to sit down, and I haven't used the wheelchair in a week. It's great to be out for the hospital."

"Do you think you're progressing faster, since being out of

the hospital?" Mr. Moore asks.

"Definitely. I have to do more for myself, so you learn to figure it out. They baby you so much in the hospital. Everything is in one room, and what isn't they bring to you. If I want food, I have to get out of the room and go get it."

"I agree. Walking around was difficult in the hospital, but once home, it got easier, when you *have* to do it." Johnny says.

They ask about my family, and before I know it, Becky pokes her head in. "Time to eat boys." We all settle in at the table, and it's weird to sit at one end with Lexi's dad at the other.

Lexi smiles, and we all start passing food fried chicken, mashed potatoes, coleslaw, cornbread, and French fries.

"This food looks delicious, angel," I lean over and tell her.

"So, where are you on the plans for this place?" Her dad asks.

"We submitted the charity paperwork and got a charity coordinator intern, who is already lining up some fundraising ideas. As you know, the blueprints are a go, thank you for that by the way." She smiles at her dad, who nods his head.

"You started designing some of the rooms, and we're under contract to buy the house next door." I finish for her.

I can't believe it's been a week since I've gotten out of the hospital. A week since we put this idea in motion, and so much has gotten done.

"Well, when you close, let me know what you want to be done in there. I want you to have a safe place to sleep, while you do all this." Her dad says in his fatherly, *'I mean what I say voice.'*

"I promise, Dad," Lexi says. "Now, Becky tell me what I have to do to get you to..."

"Yes," Becky says.

"What?" Lexi laughs.

"Johnny and I were talking, and I want to work at Oakside with you. I've been working helping servicemen and women transfer back into civilian life, so I want to do that at Oakside, whatever the pay is. Plus, working for my sister-in-law and best friend, I know she'll be flexible with her niece or nephew." Becky says, rubbing her tummy.

"I'll never know how you knew that's what I was going to ask." She laughs.

"Whatever you need, I'll volunteer my time. I figure my story might help someone." Johnny says.

Lexi looks at me and smiles. I know she's thinking what I am. It's all falling into place.

Later, once her family leaves and the kitchen is cleaned up, I step behind her at the sink and wrap my arms around her.

"Close your eyes," I whisper in her ear, and she does as I ask.

"Imagine this room is the physical therapy room. The cabinets and the window seat are gone. It's filled with exercise equipment, a desk for the therapist, and some chairs. Do you see it?"

"Yes."

"You okay with it still?" I need to know.

"More than okay with it. I promise you, Noah, when I decided to do this, I felt at peace. This is what this house was meant for, I feel it in my bones. Plus, the cabinets aren't original. The doors, wood floor, and molding that are all original is staying, my dad made sure of it." Now, why don't you go finish up the paperwork for your school, while I finish up here?"

I head back to the office to start working on the paperwork. I found a program I can do online, so I can still be here to help Lexi. I'm just finishing up when she walks in.

189

"How's it going?" She asks as I pull her into my lap.

"Just finished," I pull her in for a kiss. Lexi now has a habit of tracing my scars, when she kisses me, and it turns me on like nothing else.

When she traces the scars on my side, each touch of her hand sends an overload of sensation straight to my cock. Without breaking the kiss, she turns to straddle me, and I'm thankful this chair doesn't have wheels.

Pulling back, she removes her shirt and mine, before her lips are pressed to mine. Then, her hand is gliding over my scars tracing them. She has them memorized and knows the perfect spots to touch that make me hot, and even harder if that's possible.

I run my hand up her sides to her breasts and pinch her already hard nipples, causing her to gasp. When she starts grinding on me, I think I might lose it.

"Maybe, we should move to the bedroom," I whisper against her lips.

When she reaches into her back pocket, the last thing I expect her to pull out is a condom.

"I may have come prepared." She says with a smile and continues to kiss me.

"I think we still have way too many clothes on," I mumble between kisses.

She stands up and takes her clothes off and is frozen in front of me. This beautiful girl is naked, offering herself to me, and even from here, I see how wet she is. How wet she is for *me.*

I reach out and take the condom from her. Ripping it open and rolling it on, I don't take my eyes off of her. When I'm done, she straddles my lap again and starts rubbing her pussy on my cock, driving me crazy.

My heart is racing a million miles a minute, but I want this, I want her, and I want us. I stroke her smooth skin and run my thumbs over her breasts.

"You're so beautiful," I say, enjoying her soft skin and the contrast to my scarred body.

This time, when she slides up my cock, just the tip slides into her, causing us both to moan, before she slides back down my shaft. Her eyes meet mine, and then the tip is inside her, and slowly, she takes more and more of me, until I'm fully seated inside of her. I grab her hips and pull her towards me, grinding her clit against me, as she falls forward and buries her face in my neck.

She braces her hand on my shoulders and starts moving herself up and down my cock slowly. Already my lower back is starting to tingle, and every nerve I have is being pulled towards my cock, waiting for the tension to snap.

My heart is hammering against my chest so hard that I'm afraid it's going to burst through. My balls are drawn up and begging for release, but I don't give in until she does. I need her to climax almost more than I need to cum.

She shifts angling her legs around the back of the chair, and I sink impossibly deep inside her, and with one more stroke, she's throwing her head back, screaming my name and clenching my cock, like a vice. Her fingernails dig into my shoulders, and the pain mixed with her pussy soaking my dick, makes me cum harder than I can ever remember.

I cup the back of her neck and rest her forehead on mine.

"I love you, angel," I tell her, but is so inadequate for what I feel for her, and I'm not sure I'll ever have the right words.

Every sensation is overwhelming, when she starts tracing my scars again, a move that I think is as comforting to her, as it is becoming to me. Resting my hands on her hips, I hold her tight.

"I love you too, Noah. So much."

"I got you, angel. I got you," I tell her, as the grip on my shoulder increases.

Her head rests on my shoulder, and I hold her to me like if I let her go, she will float away. We're both breathing hard, trying to catch our breath. I can feel her heart racing just as fast as mine is.

When she lets out a content sigh, I smile.

"Normally, I'd carry you to bed and cuddle with you, angel, but that's not happening," I say, hating that I can't just yet.

"Mmm, it's okay. Just need a few minutes, because my legs are jello." She mumbles against me, and since I don't want to move either, I hold her tighter. We will get to bed eventually.

# Chapter 34

**Lexi**

What a whirlwind month it's been. We got our charity approval back faster than we expected, and now, the paperwork is with the VA, and we have already had a few people call asking questions. Judy and Keith said that's a good sign.

We closed on the house and property next door, and my dad has started renovations. He's determined to have the house ready before any work is started on Oakside, so Noah and I have a place to relax.

Johnny's been helping with the house too, and he's really happy. I took them some lunch the other day, and he was laughing and joking with the workers. He told me later they don't treat him like he's injured; they expect him to do his share of the work, missing leg or not, and that's exactly what he needs. I know construction was never his dream, but I think he's found where he fits in.

Now, we're on our way to the hospital to talk to Brooke and Easton. We're hoping we can convince them both to join us.

"First stop, Brooke?" Noah asks.

"Yeah, I think she'll be the easier one of the two."

We find her at the nurse's station. "Lexi!" She jumps up and hugs me.

"Noah! Looking great! Up and walking, look at you!" She says, taking a full survey of him.

"Would you be willing to take a walk with us?" I ask her.

"Yeah, I need some coffee anyway." She walks with us down the hall.

I decide to jump right into it.

"So, long story short. The big, old house finally showed its purpose. It's going to be a rehabilitation home for military men and women. There's one like it in Texas, and they've been helping me. We're already just waiting on final VA approval." I tell her.

"That's awesome, Lexi! Oh, there are so many guys here that I know would heal so much faster, if they weren't actually here." Her face lights up.

"Noah said that, too. He healed faster, because he had, too."

"Exactly! Oh, I'm so excited for you guys."

"Well, we want you to join us. Run the nursing staff, once we're up and running." I tell her.

Noah squeezes my hand, as I continue, "We don't need an answer now. Just think about it. If you're even slightly interested, get with me on what you would need salary wise. You'd have patients, and you'd be in charge of the small nursing staff. Hiring, training, and also, we'd want you to help in the renovations setting up things that will work best for you. All that."

"I'll talk to my family about it." She nods. "I like the idea, help get the place off the ground. Tell me what you have so far." I go on and tell her about Mandy and her fundraising ideas, and how so many people are ready to start the moment we have the okay from the military and the VA.

Once she agrees again to think about it, we head to see Easton. Noah knocks on his door, and Easton, who like always, is sitting at the window slightly turns his head.

"Hey, it's Noah, and I brought Lexi. We were hoping we could talk to you about something."

Easton turns his head a bit more to us, and Noah takes it as a yes.

"We have been working on starting up a military rehabilitation home for guys like us, who don't need to be in the hospital anymore but aren't quite ready to go home. We want you to be one of the first patients there." Noah says.

I add in softly. "It's being set up in an old plantation home, and it will be like a bed-and-breakfast. You'll have your own room, and there will be things to do, gardens, and all your treatment would be on the property. And we'll make sure your room has a great view."

"Would you be willing to move there, once we open?" Noah asks.

Easton doesn't say anything for so long that I worry he might not answer us.

"Yes, if there's a good view." He says, his deep voice scratchy.

"I promise, it will be better than the parking lot of the hospital," I say.

Easton nods and then turns back to the window.

"I'll be back next week," Noah says before we turn to leave.

With a big smile on his face, Noah says, "I don't know if we can help him, but I'm sure as hell going to try."

We get to the lobby, and I hear a familiar voice.

"Oh, Molly, don't do that!" Paisley squeals, and the next thing I know the giant golden retriever is at my feet.

195

I just laugh and lean down to pet her.

"Sorry, I guess she likes you two," Paisley says.

Just like that, an idea sparks, and I look at Noah, and I know he has the same thought.

"Paisley, do you take Molly to places other than the hospital?" I ask.

"No, I like working with military guys. Molly has a bond with them."

I give her the same run down on Oakside that we gave Brooke and watch her eyes light up.

"Would you be willing to come in with Molly, once we are up and going?"

"Oh, yes! You know, I work with therapy dogs and train them, so if there is a soldier that needs one, I'm always happy to work with them. The military will pay for the dog's training, and even help the solder with their upkeep." Paisley says, writing her cell phone number on a business card and handing it to me.

"That's good to know. We'll keep in touch." I say, taking her card and putting it in my wallet.

As we walk back to my car, Noah pulls me into his side, and I wrap my arm around his waist.

"Want to go check out the house?" He asks.

"Yeah, want to drive?" I hold out the keys.

His physical therapist said he could start driving shorter distances, since his muscles are stronger now, but no highway driving or long drives.

He takes the keys and helps me into the car, and we head home.

"I don't like driving as much, because I still need both hands, which means I can't hold your hand." He pouts.

"Well, I'm happy to drive, so we can hold hands, but you need to practice some too and get used to it," I tell him.

We pull into the driveway of what will be our new home, and I smile. The white colonial house in front of us is already feeling like home and will do even more once the construction debris is gone.

Walking into the entryway, the staircase is right in front of you, and to the right is a sliding barn door, opening to the formal dining room. Walking down the short hallway, we find my dad and my brother in the living room.

"Perfect timing, we just finished the fireplace. What do you think?" Johnny asks.

The fireplace is flanked by two floor-to-ceiling windows. The mantle is now larger and white to match the soft gray on the walls, and the entire room is so much brighter.

"I love it," I tell them.

"Kitchen is done as well. We did want to talk to you about the basement." My dad says.

"What about it?"

"Well, it's set up as a two-bedroom apartment, and it opens up to the backyard. But you don't really need a two bedroom apartment. When you come down the stairs, there's a laundry room and storage, before entry into the apartment. Any ideas what you want to do with space?" Dad asks.

"I was thinking of keeping it as it is. We won't have a place at Oakside for families to stay when they visit. Well, at least not right away, and I don't ever want a family to not be able to visit, because of a place to stay. Can we put a better door and lock on the storage, and a security door at the top of the steps? And a keypad for the entry to the basement from the outside?"

Noah wraps his arm around my waist and kisses the top of

my head. "That sounds perfect, angel."

My dad smiles and makes a note. "Okay, let's look at the kitchen. Any changes, before we move on upstairs?"

The kitchen is done in white cabinets with a gray granite countertop, and the kitchen sink overlooking the backyard. There's a breakfast nook for less formal meals that could easily seat eight. It's against a window and has a long, bench window seat at one end of the table.

"Looks great. Noah?" I ask him.

"It's perfect."

"Okay, just a few things upstairs." My dad says as we follow him.

The upstairs landing has two more window seats, and a full wall of built in bookshelves.

"We aren't touching this other than a little touch up paint, right?" My dad asks.

"Right. This is one of my favorite places in the house."

"Just need you to confirm paint colors in the bedrooms," Dad says. There are three bedrooms, plus the master up here, and they all only need touch ups. The bathrooms have recently been redone, so we aren't touching them.

"One more thing downstairs," I say.

There's a door between the living room and the formal dining room that leads to a beautiful, sun porch on the side of the property that faces Oakside, only there are so many trees you can't see Oakside.

"I'd like to make a path from here to Oakside. It needs to be as flat as possible, and I don't want it messing with Oakside's tree lined driveway, but it can lead towards where the master bedroom is now on that side of the house. It should be wide enough for a golf cart to pass a person or two. Maybe, a few benches along the way." I say. "I want patients and even staff to feel like they can come to talk to us when they need anything. So, I want it as easy as possible to get to us, if we aren't there."

"Will do. I'll see about doing some landscaping, making it a nice walk, and adding some solar lights." Dad says.

"Perfect."

Standing here in the sunroom, I start to see this place like home, and my new dream unfolding. Here's to hoping the roadblocks are few.

# Chapter 35

**Noah**

Today, we're driving to Arlington Cemetery for Tyler's birthday tomorrow. Johnny and Becky are with us, and the car is full of talking and laughter, while Johnny drives, and I sit in the back seat and get to hold my girl.

The girls are singing to the radio, and Becky is talking about having some more of the pizza they had the last time they were here.

"So, where are you with Oakside?" Becky asks.

"Well, construction has started, and the first floor is ready. They're fixing up the basement with the kitchen and offices next. While we're gone, the elevator will go in. They're expanding the second floor and all. Construction should be completed in just a few weeks, and then it's decoration time. While we work on that, we can bring patients in to the first floor rooms that are almost finished. Mom is having a ball decorating them. We have some fundraising events set up, too." Lexi says.

"Which I am not looking forward, too," I grumble.

Lexi asked me to tell my story, as the inspiration for Oakside.

Just because I agreed I'd do anything for her, doesn't mean I'm looking forward to it.

"I know, but you're the whole reason Oakside was conceived. Your story needs to be part of this." Lexi says.

"Sorry man, but I agree there," Johnny says.

"Did you know Brooke agreed to join us? She's been sorting through the applications, while still working at the hospital. We'll start interviewing staff in a week or two. We figure people will need time to give notice at their other jobs, so we want to account for that." Lexi says.

"Well, you know I'm ready. My last day was a week ago, and plan to take it easy until the baby comes and help you as needed." Becky says.

"I'm sure Mom would love help with decorating if you're up for it."

The girls launch into decorating talk until we get to the hotel. We check in and order in pizza. Johnny and Becky join us in our room, and we just talk and hang out. Everything is light and fun.

The next morning there's a change in the mood. Everyone is more serious, as we make our way to the graveyard.

Watching the Changing of the Guard at the Tomb of the Unknown Soldier is unlike anything I've ever seen. Not one person speaks during the ceremony. Once complete everyone goes their separate ways, but Lexi doesn't move.

I look over and Becky and Johnny are not sure what to do. Becky steps beside her and holds her hand. Following her lead, I take her other hand, and then pull her back to us. She offers me a small smile before we turn and start heading past rows and rows of headstones that all look exactly the same, but with different names.

When we turn down a row, and my heart starts to race, this is the man who gave everything he could. Then, from beyond the grave, he brought me my angel and gave me a reason to fight. I owe him everything.

When we stop in front of the gravestone, it reads:

Tyler Bates
 Staff Sargent, US Marine Corps
 Afghanistan. Iraq.
 July 16, 1991
 April 23, 2017
 Husband. Son. Brother.

No one says anything, and I think we are all in our own way giving respect to the memory of the man in front of us until Lexi starts laughing.

"He'd have hated this." She says grinning.

Becky laughs next, "Yeah, he would have said the only good thing about a birthday is the cake."

"He was deployed for the first time on his birthday, and I tried to find a way to send him a cake. I couldn't bake one, because it would go bad and get smushed, plus I don't think it would have made it to him. It would have either gotten lost, or someone would steal it. So, I made these cake batter truffles and sent them. He said they were good, but by the time they got to him, it was one big truffle, but he still ate them all." Lexi says.

"Well, it's so good to hear you laugh, darling." An older woman walks up with a man I assume is her husband beside her.

"Kim! What are you doing here?" Lexi rushes over and hugs

her.

"I had a feeling you would be here, and I wanted to check on you." She says.

"Kim, this is my brother, Johnny, his wife, and my best friend, Becky, and this is Noah. Everyone, this is Kim and her husband, Brett." Lexi introduces us.

"So, this is Noah. I can see the appeal. If I was younger, baby watch out," Kim playfully growls, and I know my cheeks have to be turning pink.

"But I got the best man of all right here; the one my Greg picked out for me." Kim smiles and wraps her arm around Brett's waist.

"Well, you have to stay, and then join us for dinner." Lexi says.

Kim looks at Brett, who smiles and says, "We'd love, too."

We all sit and talk, while they share stories of Tyler, and I listen to each one. Kim and Lexi share stories about the bond they have over losing their husbands.

At one point, Brett moves and sits beside me.

"It takes a strong guy to be here and listen to her talk about another guy she loves." He says.

"Yeah, but knowing he brought her to me, and chose me to take care of her, is an honor I don't think I can ever repay."

"You can by loving her hard with everything you have, and always honor his memory."

"Oh, Lexi you should tell them about Oakside," Becky says.

So, Lexi launches into Oakside's story, about her idea, and the progress we've made.

"We should be able to start taking patients in a few weeks. If everything goes right." Lexi says.

"What can we do to help?" Kim says without missing a beat.

"Oh, well, we always need volunteers, and help with fundraising are the two big ones," Lexi says.

"My niece is a grant writer out in California, and she's pretty good, but she hates the west coast. She's looking to move back this way, so I could have her contact you."

"That would be perfect."

"Okay, I'll network with the girls up here. We can set up some fundraisers, I'm sure."

Lexi leans over and hugs her. "More than that, I hope you'll make the trip down soon, so I can show it off to you. I bought the house next door, and there's an apartment with its own entrance, and you're welcome to stay."

"We'll be there." We spend another hour talking before we head out with the agreement to meet up for dinner that night. Dinner is much the same, laughing and talking of old memories and Oakside.

On the way home the next day, Lexi is driving, when I have an idea, and I look over at her, not sure how she will take it. While I'm debating about telling her, she interrupts my thoughts.

"Just tell me, Noah." She says without taking her eyes off the road.

"How did you know?"

"You start to get antsy and study me, trying to decide my mood, before telling me stuff."

Of course, Lexi can read me like an open book, and I shouldn't expect anything less at this point.

"Okay, well, I had an idea, and I don't know if you'll like it."

"Tell me." She reaches over to take my hand.

"I want to dedicate Oakside to Tyler. Put up a photo and his story on a wall in the lobby." I say, but stop as the car slows down, and Lexi pulls over to the side of the road.

Once the car is in park, Lexi bursts into tears, and I don't know what to do. I pull her into my arms, and she buries her head on my chest. I look in to the back seat, and Becky already has tears falling but offers me a wobbly smile. Johnny smiles and nods his head, before pulling Becky into his side.

"Angel, what's wrong. I can't fix it if I won't know what's wrong." I say in a bit of a panic.

"I love the idea, Noah." She takes some deep breaths, trying to get her emotions back under control.

When she finally lifts her head and looks at me, her eyes are sparkling, even though they're slightly puffy from crying.

"It's perfect, and I love the idea. I love you, Noah. Thank you for all this, coming with me, not wanting to hide Tyler, and for just being you." She leans in and kisses me.

Like she does with every kiss, her hand starts to touch the scars on the side of my face, and I don't think she even realizes she's doing it anymore.

"Lexi baby, we aren't alone," I whisper against her lips.

This makes her pull back, and she glances in the back seat.

"Sorry." She says, and her cheeks blush the sexiest shade of pink.

"When we get home, angel, when we get home."

# Chapter 36

**Lexi**

Oakside is officially up and running. We get our first five patients tomorrow, including Easton. And I can't wait. I also can't bring myself to leave Oakside and go home, and I think it's driving Noah a bit crazy. He seems more on edge tonight than normal.

"Just think, Noah. This is the last night Oakside will sit empty. There will be patients and staff here around the clock as of tomorrow." I say, standing in the lobby that feels like a huge living room.

We kept the fireplace but covered it in stones. The walls are white shiplap that really brightens up the whole space. One wall is covered in windows and overlooks a courtyard that is between the lobby and the hallway that has the library, dining room, and PT room.

There are couches and chairs along with bookcases and a TV, and I already know where their Christmas tree will go each year.

"Let's go for a walk outside and enjoy the night," Noah takes my hand.

The sun is just setting, and it casts a beautiful light over the property. We had a small garden added, but it has room to grow. We built it up with some stone walls and an iron gate to give it a hidden away, but peaceful sanctuary for patients.

On one side there's a wood arbor that by this time next year will be covered in the most beautiful flowers. Under the arbor are two large swings the size of couches that can fit up to four people easily. They have comfortable pillows on them that make them inviting.

Then, on the other side of the garden is a manmade stream that you can walk along, and even has a waterfall along with a bench you can sit next, too. There are benches scattered throughout the garden, and I can see patients out here, enjoying the sun.

We walk down no particular path until we reach the center of the garden, and Noah stops and turns to me.

"Look at everything you did, Lexi, bringing this place to life, bringing me back to life."

"Noah, you were a big help in both of those things as well."

He smiles and takes both my hands in his.

"The way I feel about you is like nothing I've ever felt. Sometimes it's scary, sometimes it's breathtaking, and other times it leaves me amazed. I love you, and I know now I didn't know what love was until I met you. Your dream for Oakside is infectious. I saw it sprouting that first day, and it took hold of me, too. I can't wait to see what you do with this place, and I can't wait to be by your side, as you do." Then, he drops down on one knee.

I gasp. This is the last thing I expected tonight. I was so wrapped up in everything happening tomorrow. Is this why Noah has been on edge all night?

"Lexi, I know we have both been here before. But I could tell you nothing has ever felt more right like if I passed this up, I'd be making the worst mistake of my life. I will love you with every breath that I have. Will you marry me, angel?"

There's no doubt in my mind when I answer him. I'm not sure when it happened, but at some point, I knew I'd spend the rest of my life by his side. When I looked into my future with him and with Oakside, I saw us together.

"Oh, Noah. I love you too, and yes, I will marry you," I throw my arms around his neck.

He slides the most beautiful emerald cut ring on my finger, before standing and pulling me into a scorching kiss. Then, with a huge smile on his face, he pulls me along to the waterfall. On the bench are a few blankets and pillows.

"Now for the record, so it doesn't come up, no, that's not the ring I gave Whitney. When I called my mom to tell her I was going to propose, she tore me up one side and down another about not using the same ring. I never got Whitney's ring back."

I just laugh, "I can see your mom doing that."

"So, this is the last night, before Oakside is never empty again. I want to make love to you here by the waterfall. What do you say, angel?" He says, looking at his feet a bit shy.

"Oh, Noah, it's perfect," I say.

He grabs the blanket and lay it down on the ground and add the pillows and place a second blanket down by our feet, as we both sit down and stare at the waterfall before he pulls me in for a kiss.

Then, he lays me back on the blanket and rolls over on top of me. Bracing himself on his elbows, he runs his hands through my hair, framing my face.

"I can't wait to see you wearing my ring and nothing else," he kisses my nose.

"I can't wait to see you wearing nothing," I say, and he smiles.

In no time flat, we remove our clothes and toss them on the bench. I lay back down on the blanket, and he takes a moment to let his eyes roam over me, and I do the same to him. This amazing, strong man is mine.

He takes his time kissing every inch of exposed skin that he can from my neck to my chest to my stomach and back up.

"Noah," I whisper.

"Taking it slow tonight, angel." He whispers back.

\* \* \*

I still can't stop staring at my engagement ring, since Noah put it there last night. Thinking of last night makes me blush. Noah did take it slow. He teased me for hours both of us hovering on the edge. It was the best night of my life.

Even now, as we stand at the Oakside front door and watch the transportation van drive up bringing our first five patients, I twist the ring to watch the light catch it. I know Noah is excited to have Easton here, and Brooke is all smiles, too. She's as excited about today as we are.

Until we take on more patients, we have a limited staff. But everyone we hired is just as excited for today as we are; they are passionate about helping our servicemen and women.

When the van parks, we all head over to help the guys out.

"Hailey, I didn't expect to see you here!" Brooke says, hugging her friend.

"I volunteered for the transport duty for this place. Figured

209

I'd take any way to see my bestie now that she's left me alone at the hospital," Hailey then hands Brooke the folder for the patients.

"Nothing has changed, since I talked to you. We did have to give Easton a sedative, so we brought a wheelchair for him." Hailey turns to us.

"You guys know Easton, but these guys are Jared, Asher, Oliver, and James."

It's a flurry of activity, getting them settled in their rooms, and the nurses as well as Noah and me, catch up on their files. We decided to be as hands on as possible. We want to know the patients and bring in specialists if needed to help them.

Someone like Easton who needs specialized treatment. I talked to Paisley, and she'll be visiting in a few weeks after she finishes training the dog she's working with. We're hoping some time with Molly might help Easton.

We spent all this time worrying about what we can bring in to help them that we didn't plan on what we need to keep out.

# Chapter 37

### Noah

Today, I wake up, and Lexi is already out of bed. Judging by the smell of coffee, I think she's downstairs in the kitchen. How she's up so early after the long night at the fundraiser last night, I don't know.

That makes the third fundraiser in two weeks, and as much as I know we need the money for Oakside, I need a break from being on display all night.

I hate waking up without her in my arms, but I get dressed, before heading downstairs, because I know Lexi will want to head over to Oakside, as soon as we are done eating.

I find Lexi at the countertop bar on her tablet drinking coffee. I walk up behind her and kiss her on the top of the head.

"Morning, angel," I say and get my coffee.

"Look, Noah, the fundraiser last night was covered by a news outlet in Atlanta."

"Great," I say, not even looking at what she shows me.

"Noah, this is really good exposure for Oakside."

"Lexi, I need a break. I can't keep doing these fundraisers like this. It's too much." I tell her straight to the point.

"But it's only been three of them." She looks up at me.

"Lexi, it's draining. Standing up there and reliving the worst thing to ever happen to me over and over. Then, I'm on display the rest of the night. It's hard enough dealing with the scars without feeling like a zoo animal. Then, there's people asking questions they have no business asking me all night long." I set my coffee down without even drinking it.

"Noah…"

"No, Lexi, how would you like to have to tell the story of the day two uniformed officers showed up on your doorstep to tell you Tyler was dead? How you had to bury Tyler? Would you like to have to tell that story over and over and over, and then answer questions to complete strangers all night?"

"I wouldn't," she whispers.

"Exactly. I'm heading in. See you there." I escape to Oakside.

Oakside has become my sanctuary. Here I'm surrounded by people who get it, and no one looks twice at my scars. The walk from our house next door down the path to Oakside is enough to clear my heart and get me in a better mood.

The guys here have enough to deal with, and they don't need me in a crappy mood from things going on in my life. I want to give them my all, so the walk gets me in the headspace to do just that.

Like I do every day, my first stop is to see Easton. He's talking to me a little more, but not anyone else. I knock on his door, and he doesn't even need to turn from the window.

"Noah," he says.

"Hey, how are you doing today?" I ask him like I do every morning.

"Same as yesterday. What's wrong?" One thing I learned about Easton is he might be quiet, but he picks up on everything.

"Lexi and I had an argument before I came over. It's hard doing these fundraisers and telling my story all the time." I'm honest with him.

"I can imagine. Maybe, it's time to share someone else's story. Wasn't her bother injured in the same blast?"

Of course, a simple solution. Johnny keeps saying he wants to help out and do more. He can fill in for the next fundraiser or two, and it would give me enough of a break, before the big one on the schedule in Knoxville.

I smile, "Yeah, he was. Thank you."

"Noah?"

"Yeah?"

"Give Lexi a bit more time to cool down."

I laugh, "You're right, and I will. I'll be back around later."

Easton nods, and that's the end of our visit. I make my rounds and check on the other guys here. Most are happy to be here, but some not so much. I check in with the staff to make sure they have what they need, before going to find Lexi. Normally, she's working at the desk in the lobby, available in case anyone needs her.

As I walk into the lobby, I almost run into Lexi, but she looks even madder than she did, when I left the house. I want to smooth things over, but I guess Easton is right this isn't the time. But this seems to be more than just our fight this morning.

"What's wrong?" I place a hand on her shoulder.

She doesn't shrug my hand away, so that's something, but she doesn't speak. She just points to Whitney at the other end of the lobby.

"I'll tell her to leave."

"Noah, talk to her. You need closure, and she obviously has something to say. You guys have a history."

She won't meet my eyes, and I detect a quiver in her voice.

I don't want Lexi to ever feel like the door on Whitney isn't closed, and even though I have no desire to ever talk to her again, I will for Lexi.

"Okay, but only because you told me, too." I try to tilt her head up to look at me, but she won't budge.

"I have things to do," she says, walking away.

I watch her go and want nothing more than to chase after her and fix this now because I hate having her upset at me. But I have to get rid of Whitney first. She always did have a knack for bad timing.

"Noah!" She says loudly, as soon as she sees me and tries to hug me, which I dodge. There are a few people scattered around the lobby, so I know this isn't the place to do this.

"Hey, let's go to the courtyard and talk."

The courtyard will get her away from the patients but isn't really private either.

"Lead the way." Whitney smiles that fake for the public smile.

I take her to the lobby door that opens to the courtyard, walking over to a bench, and sit on the edge. She then sits down as close as she can get. My whole body goes stiff. I don't like her close. Heck, I don't like anyone, but Lexi this close.

Her perfume makes my stomach roll, and I'm ready for this to be over all ready.

"What are you doing here, Whitney?"

"I've been thinking about you a lot, Noah. Things... Things didn't end well, and that's on me. The stress of it all it was too much."

"You don't think I was under stress?" I grit out. "I was lying in a hospital bed fighting for my life."

"I know you were, Noah. I know that now, but look what you've done." She looks around the courtyard, making me hate that she's here in this space.

"I wanted to come and apologize. I handled things horribly." She makes it actually sound sincere.

"You did, but it all worked out," I say, keeping my voice flat and free of emotion.

She looks down at her hands in her lap, and when she looks back up at me, her eyes are teary, but I have an inkling they're fake and forced.

"We could be great together, Noah. This place is an amazing concept, and with the right push, it could be huge. Think about it. With my influence and you on my arm, it would really elevate Oakside into something great. Give us another chance, Noah." She says, resting her hand on my arm.

Whitney is an influencer on social media; she's a ladder climber, ambitious, too. When I was in the hospital, the more I thought about it, the more I think she was with me to have a military connection. A soldier on her arm for photos to make her look good. Also saying she's a military girlfriend or fiancé to get publicity or anything else free she could get out of it.

It's why she was so obsessed about the photos and so sure I'd ruined them. Now, she wants to waltz back in here, as if nothing happened.

She misreads my silence and keeps talking.

"You know I love you. I always have. I want to support you in this." She pouts with what I'm sure she thinks is sexy.

I laugh. I don't mean to, but I don't know what other emotion to show right now.

"No, that's not love. You see what I've made of myself, and

215

you want to latch on for the ride. I never loved you, I know that now. What I have with Lexi is love. She was there in my worst moments and never turned her back on me. She gave me a reason to fight. What I feel with her is ten times more powerful than anything I ever felt with you. I don't hold a grudge against you, but I'm not seeing us ever being on friendly terms either. I know this is a big publicity stunt because you love the limelight." I get it all off my chest.

I guess Lexi was right, I did need the closure.

"Fuck you, Noah." She says now pissed, jumping up from the bench.

"You already fucked me over, but it's okay because it brought me my angel. Lexi is the light of my life, and she agreed to marry me, because she loves me for me, scars and all. You can leave now, Whitney, and don't show your face here again. You aren't welcome."

# Chapter 38

### Lexi

I hate that Noah walked out of the house today mad. I hate that we didn't work it out before we came over to Oakside for the day. And most of all, I hate that he's now out there talking to that plastic Barbie wannabe.

As I stand in the Lobby and watch Noah in the courtyard with Whitney, Brooke walks up beside me.

"Who is that?"

I fill her in on Noah and Whitney's brief history of that day in the hospital in Germany.

"So, what's she doing here?"

"I don't know, but stupid me encouraged him to go talk to her, making sure he got closure, but now I'm second guessing it all." I begin spinning my engagement ring around on my finger.

"What do you have to doubt? We all know that man loves you beyond reason. If this girl is as horrible as you say she is, what do you have to worry about?"

"Honestly, first loves are intense and hard to get over. I'm worried she'll want him back, and he might want to try again.

They have a long history."

"I will kick his ass myself. You were there for him every day. I can't remember the last time I saw someone who devoted that much attention to the guys in the hospital. There are wives who didn't spend near as much time with their husbands. He has to know that."

I watch Whitney look at her hand, and her bottom lip trembles, before she looks back up at him.

"She's sitting so close, yet, he hasn't moved away. The only other person he lets that close to him is me."

"I bet he doesn't want to be rude." She says, but her reasoning sounds flat.

"Maybe," but when he laughs, my heart sinks.

Brooke must know I'm ready to bolt because she wraps an arm around my waist and pulls me to her side. It's like a train wreck. I know what I'll see is going to break my heart, but I can't look away no matter how hard I try.

"I wanted to send her on her way and not tell him. I wanted to tell him no don't talk to her, just make her go away, but this is a choice that he has to make." I sigh, resting my head on her shoulder.

"Yeah, it is. But standing here can't be good for you either." Brooke tries to pull me away back towards the patient rooms, and just as I'm about to go, Whitney jumps up from the bench, and she looks all kinds of pissed. Like I'm being pulled by some invisible force, I'm at the door and cracking it open just enough to hear what's being said. Brooke follows and stands right behind me.

Noah's voice fills the air. "You already fucked me over, but it's okay because it brought me my angel. Lexi is the light of my life, and she agreed to marry me, because she loves me for me, scars and all. You can leave now, Whitney, and don't show your face here again. You aren't welcome."

Relief like I've never known washes over me, and I almost sag to the ground.

"You're engaged *again*?" Whitney screeches, and how she makes the word again sound dirty, I have no idea.

"Well, you sure as fuck move on fast. Wonder how long your engagement will last this time." She snaps.

"After several years, I proposed to you, because it felt like the next step. I proposed to Lexi after less than a year, because I know I can't live without her, and there's a huge difference." Noah's voice is even, and I know he's restraining himself.

Something in his words kills the irritation, self-doubt, and anger from earlier today. This is my Noah, and I need to stop doubting him.

In the next moment, all I can think about is getting her out of here, because her yelling is the last thing the guys need. Looking around the lobby, the only person available to help me is Brooke.

"We have to kick her out," I say, trying to formulate a plan.

"Lexi, call the cops. If nothing else, you'll want it on record she isn't allowed on these grounds."

Trusting her advice, I pull out my phone and explain the situation and dispatch says a car is on its way. I tell her they can walk right in, as we aren't a private residence anymore.

Then, I turn back to Noah and Whitney, who is still going on and on, but I haven't heard anything she's said, and judging by Noah's eyes on me, he hasn't either.

"Ready?" I say to Brooke.

"Yep, with any luck, we can get her out front."

I step into the courtyard with Brooke behind me.

"It's time for you to leave, Whitney. The guys here can be triggered by your hissy fit, and that will put you and everyone else here at risk," I say my tone as flat as I can manage.

"I'm talking to Noah. This doesn't concern you." She spits out.

When her eyes land on my engagement ring, I know she realizes who I am.

"Actually, it does, because I own this place, as does Noah. He asked you to leave, and now I'm telling you to leave."

"This doesn't concern you. I am talking to Noah." She tries talking to me like I'm a child, who doesn't understand what she's saying.

"It does concern her because she's my fiancée," Noah says, walking to my side and wrapping an arm around my waist, and just like that, everything feels right with us again.

"Cops are here," Brooke says and heads to the lobby to meet them.

"You called the cops!" Whitney screeches.

Noah chuckles silently beside me.

"Yes, because like I said, you acting like this, can trigger some of the men, and I wasn't going to chance it," I say just as Brooke steps into the courtyard with the two uniformed officers.

We spend the next thirty minutes explaining who Whitney is, what Oakside is, and why her throwing a fit can cause problems. I explain how both Noah and I asked her to leave, and she just threw a bigger tantrum.

We were asked some questions, mostly about Oakside to get the place in the system in case we call again. Then, they'd have more information on what they were walking into.

Whitney is carted off and warned not to step foot on the property again.

Noah and I stand in the front yard, watching the cops leave, and Noah pulls me into his side. As we head back to the porch, I see Easton in the window. He nods his head as almost a thank you for the show, and I smile at him and wave. He doesn't wave back, but I didn't expect him, too.

"I kind of thought about snapping a video of her hissy fit and tagging her for all her '*fans*' to see." I laugh, as we make our way to the front porch.

"I don't think I'd have stopped you. I do need to send her an official letter to take all my photos down and to stop using me as her military affiliation." Noah sighs.

I turn to him then.

"I'm so sorry about this morning. I was so focused on this place that I stopped focusing on us, but something about seeing you with Whitney today," I can't find the words, so I just shake my head.

"Angel, we're going to argue, and we aren't always going to agree. That is what will keep things interesting. I love you and no fight changes that. I want this place to succeed too, and it's just a matter of balance. Easton actually had an idea of what I was coming to talk to you about when the whole Whitney thing happened." He says, as he leads me over to one of the rocking chairs and sits down, before pulling me into his lap.

"Yeah?" I ask.

"It doesn't always have to be me speaking at these events. There are a few local ones, so let's ask your brother to speak. Then, I'll go with you to Knoxville, and we can take a weekend there and have a mini vacation."

"That sounds good," I snuggle into him. "We really need to look at getting security on site."

"Yeah, I was thinking that, too. Easton would be perfect if

221

we can get through to him." He says.

"If anyone can, it would be you, Noah. I know it. He's already closer to you than anyone else." I say pausing. "Noah, what if I don't want to wait to get married?"

"What do you mean?"

"We're so busy that planning something right now would be too hard. What if we flew my family out to your family for a weekend and just did a simple courthouse wedding? Then, once things have settled here, we can renew our vows and have a big event." I say, but not lifting my head to look at him.

"I say let's do it, but I do have one request."

"What's that?"

"I want you in a white dress. I have been dreaming of you walking down the aisle to me in a white dress."

"I can make that happen."

# Chapter 39

**Lexi**

*6 months later*

I can't believe Oakside has been in operation for over six months now. Time has flown by.

Noah's sisters have taken over my food websites with the condition that 10% of the profits come back to Oakside, and they both still go to college. They have done some great things with it, and it's growing faster than I was able to get it over the last year.

Johnny has done quite a few local fundraisers, giving Noah a break from them. He loves doing them, so that's a plus. Noah went with me to the Knoxville fundraiser, and we met Owen and Ellie there.

Owen owns several major companies in the city, and I looked up his net worth, and it was over a billion dollars. My jaw dropped because he's so down to earth. Ellie and I hit it off, and the donation we got from Owen alone was more than we received from all the last fundraisers we put on. It was enough to give us some breathing room and finish up the main building, fully staff the place, and get some plans drawn up for the barn.

Thanks to them we now have all twenty-one rooms open and ready. Eighteen of them are filled, and the last three are taken just waiting for the hospital to release the guys to us.

Ellie and Owen are here now, staying with us, along with their two little girls. They took the grand tour of the property yesterday, and Ellie wants to get hands on today, so she's shadowing Brooke. Owen is going to work with Noah, and I have the girls who want to do some craft projects for the guys.

There hasn't been a peep from Whitney, since the day the cops took her away. Just as we talked about that day, we flew my family out to Noah's family and had a small courthouse wedding the weekend before we went to Knoxville, so we used Knoxville as our honeymoon.

"Daddy!" The girls squeal and jump up from the table, where they were making cards.

I didn't notice Owen and Noah walk in, but Noah is smiling and makes his way over to sit down with me.

"Owen just wrote us another check. He said to put it aside and use it to sponsor someone who needs help, who the insurance won't cover."

"You told him?" I ask.

Last month, we had to turn away our first patient. They had been out of the military for a while, and the fight with insurance landed them in not being covered.

"Maybe, we can reach out and get them in the next open room we have," I say, thinking out loud.

"Sounds good to me," Noah says.

After a day of showing Owen and Ellie around, they head out to do some sightseeing, and Noah and I go home.

"You enjoyed being around those girls today," Noah says more as a statement.

"Yeah, I did."

"I don't see Oakside slowing down anytime soon. We have a great staff, though."

"What are you saying?"

"Why don't we stop preventing pregnancy and just see what happens? There's never going to be a perfect time, angel. But we can make it work."

My heart races. This is the dream I gave up so long ago. For the longest time, I only imagined having kids with Tyler. Then, I settled on not having kids at all, or maybe even adopting. But lately, more and more of the dream is back, but this time with Noah.

I've sat up at night thinking of Noah as a father. He's going to make a great one. I imagine a baby boy, looking just like his dad. The kids growing up being proud of their dad, knowing what a hero he is.

"Are you sure?" I ask him.

"I want kids with you, Lexi. A little girl running around with your blonde hair."

"A little boy who looks just like his daddy," I add.

"What do you say, angel. Ready for our next adventure?"

"Yeah, I am." I smile.

This man brought me back to life, and then showed me I wasn't living like I thought I was. He has made all my dreams come true, even the newest ones.

Now, he's taken the last one and just handed it to me.

Yeah, I can't wait to go on this adventure with him, too.

# Epilogue

### Easton

You tend to appreciate the warmth of the sun hitting your face after you spend an entire year without seeing even a hint of sunlight.

I have to give it to Noah this place is much nicer to look at than the hospital parking lot. The huge oak trees lining the driveway make a great view from my room. I have a prime view of those coming and going every day.

Oakside is smaller than the hospital, and I know most of the people here, so I feel safer. Everyone respects my boundaries, including the patients.

When you are kept in a damn cold, dark room and tortured by anyone who comes near you, well, you tend not to want people in your space. I'm getting better, slowly. Much more slowly than the fancy doctors here would like. But they still give me my space.

Noah is the one who has kept pushing. Pushing me to talk, which I do more of now. Pushing me outside of the hospital room, so now, I'm in a room that looks like a fancy bed-and-breakfast. For sure, a step up.

But I can't seem to get myself out of this cage I feel like I'm in. As long as I'm here by the window with the sun in my face, it keeps the terror of that year away. Even rainy days help. because you forget how perfect rainy days truly are when you haven't seen them in a year. I wouldn't even mind the snow.

I've gotten used to all the sounds here, but I can't seem to place the scratchy clack-clack sound, coming down the hall. It's almost like light high heels, but four legs, and not two.

Before I can figure it out, a dog is in front of me and rests his or her head on my lap, and then looks up at me with these big old puppy dog eyes. He or she is a golden retriever, and while I don't like people touching me, I find I don't mind the dog.

Judging by the pink collar, I'm guessing it's a her, so I reach down and pet her. That's when I hear it.

"Molly, you can't run off like that, girl."

I know that voice. I'd recognize that voice anywhere.

It's the voice that kept me going during my year in a dark room.

*Paisley.*

\* \* \*

You can read Easton and Paisley's story in **book two of the Oakside Military Heroes, Saving Easton**. This is a brother's best friend military romance.

\* \* \*

Want Ellie and Owen's story? Read their fake relationship, age gap, steamy romance in **Accidental Sugar Daddy.**

\* \* \*

**Want Johnny and Becky's story? Get it free when you join my newsletter!**

**Get Johnny and Becky's story now.**

\* \* \*

# Connect With Kaci Rose

Website
Facebook
Kaci Rose Reader's Facebook Group
Instagram
Twitter
Goodreads
Book Bub
Amazon
Join Kaci Rose's VIP List (Newsletter)

# Other Books By Kaci Rose

See all of Kaci Rose's Books

**Oakside Military Heroes Series**
**Saving Noah** – Lexi and Noah
**Saving Easton** – Easton and Paisley
**Saving Teddy** – Teddy and Mia
**Saving Levi** – Levi and Mandy

**Chasing the Sun Duet**
**Sunrise**
**Sunset**

**Rock Springs Texas Series**
The Cowboy and His Runaway – Blaze and Riley
The Cowboy and His Best Friend – Sage and Colt
The Cowboy and His Obsession – Megan and Hunter
The Cowboy and His Sweetheart – Jason and Ella
The Cowboy and His Secret – Mac and Sarah
Rock Springs Weddings Novella
Rock Springs Box Set 1-5 + Bonus Content
The Cowboy and His Mistletoe Kiss – Lilly and Mike
The Cowboy and His Valentine – Maggie and Nick
The Cowboy and His Vegas Wedding – Royce and Anna

The Cowboy and His Angel – Abby and Greg
The Cowboy and His Christmas Rockstar – Savannah and Ford
The Cowboy and His Billionaire – Brice and Kayla

**Mountain Men of Whiskey River**
Take Me To The River
Take Me To The Cabin

**Standalone Books**
Stay With Me Now
Texting Titan
Accidental Sugar Daddy
She's Still The One

**Please leave a review on your chosen retailer!**

Made in the USA
Coppell, TX
22 June 2023

18383362R00134